SOME KIND OF ANIMAL

I broke a new Christian Brothers hockey stick. I broke it on somebody's head. He was a team-mate of mine. A friend, sort of, someone I pass to occasionally. It was only practice. There was some blood, but I think he was all right. The funny part is I don't really remember being that angry.

It was an accident, and that's that. But none of my teammates will talk to me.

It was an accident because I'm an excellent hockey player, a lot better than the guy whose bell I rang. I feel bad about it, but I bet another guy would feel a lot worse. It's like I know, in my head, that I feel bad, but I don't quite feel, in my guts, that I feel bad.

The kid screamed at me, when he got his marbles back, that I was too violent for hockey. Too violent? For hockey? What's left if you're too violent for hockey? The zoo? The electric chair?

Also by Chris Lynch:

Shadow Boxer
Gypsy Davey
Slot Machine

ICEMAN

CHRIS LYNCH

HarperTrophy®
A Division of HarperCollinsPublishers

Harper Trophy® is a registered trademark
of HarperCollins Publishers Inc.

Iceman
Copyright © 1994 by Chris Lynch
Printed in the United States of America. For information address
HarperCollins Children's Books, a division of HarperCollins Publish-
ers, 10 East 53rd Street, New York, NY 10022.

Library of Congress Cataloging-in-Publication Data
Lynch, Chris.
   Iceman / Chris Lynch.
      p.   cm.
   Summary: Fourteen-year-old Eric, a ruthless hockey player prone to
violence on the ice, tries to reconcile his own needs with those of his
parents.
   ISBN 0-06-023340-0. — ISBN 0-06-023341-9 (lib. bdg.)
   ISBN 0-06-447114-4 (pbk.)
   [1. Hockey—Fiction.   2. Parent and child—Fiction.]   I. Title.
PZ7.L979739Ic   1994   93-7776
[Fic]—dc20   CIP
                                                                  AC

◆

First Harper Trophy edition, 1995.

To Tina,
for making it possible for me to be juvenile

CONTENTS

FIRST PERIOD

PLAYING WITH FIRE

THIS IS WHY I'M CONFUSED. I'm a hockey player—a very good hockey player, not a great hockey player. My brother Duane was a great hockey player when he played, but he gave it up. "If I know one thing in this world, then this is the thing I know," he told me the day he bestowed his old equipment on me. "The minute you start thinking about the *meaning* of sports, you're useless as an athlete."

But that's not why I'm confused. I don't question why I'm a hockey player, I just am one. It's my style that's the issue. I play hard. Rock-'em sock-'em, you might say. Yet I always lead my team in scoring. Not because I've worked to develop my shot or my puck-handling skills, but because I either intimidate guys into giving the puck up to me or I ram the guy with the puck right into the net.

It works. Coach is always using me for an example

in practice. "The guy with the fire in the belly," he calls me. "If you all played with half the fire this guy has, we'd win the damn Stanley Cup." But then he'll turn around and tell them, "He's cold as ice, this boy. And that's what you need to do the job. He'd skate right over his own mother, slice her to bits, to get that puck." And he meant it as a good thing.

Somehow, he was right both ways. I'm known to other players as the Iceman, because I'm heartless. But they couldn't really know about the burning inside. Could I be both, fire and ice?

Sure, depending on the day.

Opening day this season, in my grubby little league, I was on fire. I don't play anything, don't really *do* anything, in the summer, so I was kind of itchy when the season started. I came out like a pinball, hitting everything in sight. I play defense, but right off the opening face-off I took a run at the center, leaving him flat like a bull's-eye in the face-off circle. The puck dribbled off to his left winger, who I chased, caught, and body slammed. As I sat on that guy, the defenseman came rushing by and scooped up the puck. Whoosh, he blew by the lame center and lame right winger on my team. Swoosh, he blew by our lame right defenseman.

But by the time he reached the right circle in front of our lame goalie, I was right on his ear. He heard me—I know, because when I come up behind a guy, I use a heavy, pounding stride that cuts the ice so hard you can hear it in the stands. As I hoped, he tilted a glance just slightly over his shoulder in my direction and hesitated before winding up, and he was mine. His skates left the ice momentarily as I drove him with a football-like tackle, past the net and into the boards with a crash of sticks and pads and skates. Almost knocked myself out in the process.

I dragged myself wheezing and hunching to the bench. Less than a full minute into the season, and I was so exhausted I couldn't speak.

"Sometimes I think maybe you should just leave your stick on the bench when you go out there," Coach said, laughing, as he passed me the Gatorade squeeze bottle.

That was pretty much how that first game went. I knew that I should have been pacing myself, but it was like I had no control over it. I'd sit on the bench, get my wind back, then go out like a maniac for sixty seconds, destroying everything out there until I could barely crawl back to the bench. Somehow in all that I managed to steamroll a goal in, by slashing at the goalie's hands so much in a pileup that I swear I heard him mutter, "Screw this," as he pulled his hands back. We won 1–0, mostly because by halfway through the second period nobody on their team was too hot for holding the puck, and because I was being too disruptive for my own team to get any flow going when I was on the ice. When I *wasn't* on the ice? Let's just say my team wasn't very deep, which is why I had to concentrate on staying on the ice longer, not burning out.

Game 2 was a whole different thing. Pacing was never a problem. It came only three days after that first crazy game, but I felt so different, it was like I was a different player inside the same #4 uniform. I was cool, cold even, as I thumped up and down the ice, doing my job, stopping everybody who came my way, clearing the puck out of the defensive zone, even managing to whistle a few drives on net from the point. But I felt *nothing*. I knocked some guys down with good clean checks. Some guys knocked me down. But we all went on our way. When the second period came, I had no recollection of the first and had to look up at the scoreboard to find out that we were down 2–0.

The only time I felt a little bit of a something was when I had to go with Dice. Darren Dice, a big mother of a guy who had been dogging me since my earliest peewee games, was stalking me for the first of our many annual brawls, but I hadn't even noticed him. Not much of a talent, Dice, but always with a mean stupid grin that scares people into making mistakes for him. And he could knock out a bronze statue if you let him catch you.

I was a little lazy, carrying the puck up ice early in the third period. Dice must have been in his sneaky crouch, hunting me down from all the way across the ice, because I never even saw him before he blasted me from the side. It was a perfect shoulder check that sent me headfirst into the Plexiglas by my own bench. Nice hit, I thought, and that was it—that's how dead zone I was. Until I got up and found him right in my face, both gloves off and stretching his fingers out. With the grin.

For the first time, though, I was looking almost straight into his eyes, and I filled nearly the same amount of space as him. In past years, boy had I taken some spankings from *him*.

The key, with Dice, with big guys, with tough guys, is to keep them off balance. I dropped my gloves and quickly grabbed the neck of his shirt. Using a stiff-arm technique, I jerked him first left, then right, then straight down as if I was going to ram his face on my knee. I got him so that he didn't know where he was going with each tug. But *I* knew. When I moved him to one side with my right hand— *crack!*—my left fist was there to meet his face. When I moved him to the other side, or down, or pushed him straight back, one-two-three-four-five, my left hand was like a baseball bouncing off his cheekbone, his forehead, squishing into his nose. I dissected him, hitting him exactly where and when I wanted to. All the while he had to keep scrambling just to keep his skates under him. The feeling of power, of total control, made me want to do it more, and hit him again, which I did and did.

Finally I knocked him off his feet, not so much with the punches—he *was* one tough mother—but with the constant shaking and pulling him every which way. He never even got to throw a punch. I rolled on top of him, and when the refs pulled me off, old Dice looked a little stunned. Stunned, but still smiling as much as ever, as he had through the whole fight.

I did my time in the penalty box, and by the time I got out, there was only a minute left in the game. That's what happens to guys who fight in the third period, they're basically out of it. But I didn't mind. I stayed on the ice that entire final minute and didn't contribute much. I even allowed some weenie, weasly little winger to slip past me and score a goal, making the final 4–0. But after he finished celebrating, on his next trip down ice, I wrecked him. He was flying by me, trying to do the same thing again, only this time I wasn't asleep at the wheel. I let him think he was past when, at the last instant, I threw myself sideways. I caught him perfectly in the solar plexus with my shoulder, making him suck for air so hard it sounded like a little scream. I followed through on my check, like you're supposed to, bouncing him off the boards. His stick flew into our bench. His helmet rolled fifty feet away. When the buzzer sounded to end the game, he lay on his side curled up like a cooked shrimp.

That was my job. I was doing my job. Half the crowd whooped—my father being the whoopiest— but the other half booed me. It was a *home* game, and they booed me. They didn't understand that even though the game was over, we still had to play these guys two more times this season, and this guy had to remember me. All they knew was that he was smaller than me. I didn't like doing it. But I didn't not like it, either.

That's basically how the whole season went. I'd blow hot and cold all year, from game to game. Some days I wanted to take everybody's head off and win games all by myself. Other games I just wasn't there. Thing is, I think on the outside it all looked the same to people, the way I played. I was always the Iceman, and I was the only one who knew the difference, so maybe it didn't really matter.

AND SO I RAN

"**S**HE KNOWS YOU WEREN'T AT SCHOOL again today," Duane said from the front steps as I walked up. I had my long hockey bag slung over my shoulder.

"I was sick," I said.

"You played hockey," he said.

"I was feeling better," I said. "C'mon, Duane. You were a jock once. You know how it is."

"Sorry, little bro, I can't relate. I'm pro-school now. That athletic nonsense was a million years ago."

It wasn't a million years ago, it was three. Duane has an exaggeration habit. Everything he's ever seen or done is bigger, faster, louder, scarier, meaner, daringer, smarter, dumber, funnier, sadder, longer, or purpler than could ever be possible. But I usually understood him.

Sports died for Duane when he went to high school. Everything changed then. At least it did for him and Dad. Almost from the minute he became a freshman, Duane stopped doing anything that made Dad happy. No hockey, no football. And he was good, too. With one leg, he could have played on every varsity team the high school had. But he went to the freshman football tryouts for two days, and that was it. He sold all his gear—Dad always bought us our own equipment, the finest stuff. He sold it to some kid he said probably wouldn't make the team, but the kid figured great gear would put him over the top. Then Duane took the money and bought a used Fender Stratocaster. That's a guitar.

"*The* guitar," he pointed out to me as he strummed it, his feet on the kitchen table. "Boy, in two days of moronic football tryouts, not a single one of those little frosh boys brought me down. Not one. Back and forth and back and forth I carried the stupid football down the field, then carried it back again. I was *dying* to have somebody tackle me."

"Awesome, Duane," I said. At the time that's what I thought it was, awesome. I was eleven. It was a long three years ago.

"Awesome, my butt. All I could think about the whole time I was there, running over these spastic pimple cases, was this. Was playing music. It was like some kind of religion thing, because, you know, I never played one of these in my life. But running around on that crappy field they use for freshman football and I don't know what else—cattle grazing, probably—I knew that I had to play this thing and that all this other crap of football and lacrosse and baseball and hockey was for the damn birds."

I, being up to my forehead in 'football and hockey and all the very same crap as my brother, with him as my primary model, was pretty well thrown here. He left me like one of those freshman weenies he was talking about trampling against his will. But I was completely cool with it, compared to Dad.

"What the *hell* is that?" Dad said as he came through the kitchen door. I was looking right into his pale, V-shaped face. Duane's back was to him.

Duane first yanked his feet off the table, scared out of reflex. Then he stood, turned with the Strat hanging like a shield between him and our father. The guitar was white, with an orange sunburst plate on the front. Duane's perfect, black, square Marine crew cut didn't fit the picture quite right.

"Duane, son, where did you get that?" Dad said coldly, dropping his hat and briefcase on the table. I pulled a banana out of the fruit basket on the counter and got busy peeling it.

"I bought it, Dad," Duane said, friendly, but like he was expecting something.

Even more slowly now, Dad said, "Get the money out of the bank, did you? Without discussing it with me?" It wasn't that we didn't have money of our own.

Dad saw to it that we did, but he had his finger on every drop that flowed.

Duane smiled. It was an unfamiliar smile to me then, but not so now. Just a shade nervous, but a smile that was very real and sure too. "Sold my gear, Dad," he said.

I took my banana and booted to the living room.

"Your . . . what?" His voice was deep, like a record played too slowly.

"My football junk. Pads, helmet, Nike cleats, all of it. No need for it. I walked. I'm out."

In the next room I leaned back, trying to bury myself in the overstuffed chair. This was new territory. Duane had never done anything against Dad's wishes. Neither did I. Neither *have* I. We had never even considered anything other than what he wanted. Until Duane had his vision on the football field.

I waited for the next sound to come from the kitchen. I expected it to be a loud one. But it was more. After a long, furious half minute of nothing, the next thing I heard was Duane strumming easily on his guitar. I figured that would *have* to be the detonator. Dad was going to blow. I'd never seen that, don't know why I expected it, didn't know what it would look like, but I was certain that was where we were.

No. Next thing, Duane was walking by me, a little more bounce in his step than usual. Right there, that day, that place, Duane somehow had picked up a level of cool, of control, that he'd never had before, and that he's never given up since. He was finger picking and giving me a wink on the way to his room. When still nothing seemed to be happening in the kitchen, I went in, scared.

I found my father hunched over the kitchen table, staring at his fingers spread wide and flat. He looked up at me weakly, wounded, speechless, paralyzed. I couldn't understand it, how he looked so broken, like a great friend had been taken from him. Without speaking, he lowered his head again, and I backed out of the room.

It never seemed to matter that Duane had gone from great athlete/mediocre student to turning that equation on its head. Dad always acted like he was wasting his life. That was why I always felt like I could do anything I wanted to, as long as I kept playing, and everything would be all right. Ma, unfortunately, didn't quite see it that way.

"Ma doesn't give a rat's ass if you went to hockey," Duane reminded me, even though that thought really never left me. "She knows you need saving, puck head, and she's gonna save you before it's too late."

"No, Duane, don't say it . . ."

"Oh yes, Godless Iceman."

"She's gonna Bible me."

"She's gonna Bible you legless."

I'd just come from an afternoon in which, if you touched the puck, I confronted you. If you checked me, I confronted you. If you tried to skate away from me, I confronted you. Now my mother wanted to confront me.

And so I ran. I dumped my gear on Duane, and in that light breathy rain that always strokes my forehead and calms me, I ran. I ran my regular route, no from and no to exactly, even though I always go the same way. It's just for the run. Down to the Muddy River, where I travel along the water's edge where the green pollen washes up like soapsuds, where the willow trees bend right over me like long fingers dipping in the water, where my shoes make a loud *sluck-sluck* noise as I struggle through the soup, tensing all my leg muscles to the max. Then I turn onto the narrow, twisting parkway, where there isn't any sidewalk in spots, where every tree has a big fender-height scar, and every driver who speeds by gets a sudden petrified look as he sees me and jerks the wheel in the other direction. I always run against traffic so not to miss that. Then I run through the old abandoned seminary where I used to spend every day playing baseball, but now it looks like a Mediterranean ghost town, overgrown and cracking stucco buildings that now house rats and raccoons instead of short fat guys in dresses. Then I run past the double team that haunts me, always pulls my stare like I've never seen them before—the funeral home and the cemetery. Gets to be more of a steeplechase than a marathon as I scale the eight-foot seminary wall and run down through the cemetery, hurdling stone after stone after stone with the names of all the O'Donnells and Machellis and Ortizes flying beneath me until I don't have enough spring in me to clear even one more. And to the Arboretum, past placqued trees from Japan and Nova Scotia, over hills that are like running straight up the side of a building. When the last, biggest hill crests, I pick up steam and a pack of eight or ten dogs that hang there, until it feels like we're doing eighty, me and my dogs, and I just explode back through the big wrought-iron gate, onto the street for the last quarter mile toward home again.

I don't jog this, or cruise, I run. I run every step as if it's the last leg of the 4 x 100 meter relay. When I'm done, I'm always spent, legs like overdone pasta, my brain humming like an air conditioner. More than hockey, my run runs me down, nice. That's peace. That's what peace is.

My mother used to be a nun. She quit after a couple of years to have a family which, to her disappointment, turned out to be: my father, who she sees as a bug; my older brother, Duane, who she sees as Lucifer; and me, who she sees as a project, the way somebody else might look at refinishing an old table or crocheting an afghan—something to get intense about when the mood strikes but most of the time to just let lie there. Duane says she never really quit the nuns but went into semiretirement, since she still goes to mass daily, reads the Bible for fun, and has made herself into something of a theology scholar. I don't think all that is so bad. Everybody needs a hobby. In fact I wish she'd do more of it so that she could leave me alone. My problem with her is that she says the word LOVE approximately seven billion times a week, and every single time she's quoting somebody else.

"Your problem, Eric," she said when I finally came home after running seven miles on top of hockey and blistering both feet, "is that you've lost all sense of community." She starts more conversations with "Your problem is . . ." than she does with "Hello." She held out her Bible in her left hand and pointed at it with her right. "*This* is what community is all about." She thumped the book. "*This* is where you will learn about the healing power of getting together and sharing yourself with others." She handed me the book and, to my surprise, stopped talking.

"That's it?" I said.

"Read it," she ordered. "And on Sunday, you're coming back to the church with me."

Duane walked in, laughing and strumming his guitar. "He's got community, Ma. He lives in his room with rodents and reptiles, he is a member with full privileges of the Smithsonian Associates, and he runs with a pack of wild dogs up in the park. They're very communal, you know."

"Not now, Duane," she said. "We're having a serious discussion here about something that's of absolutely no interest to you." She was very intimidated by Duane, which he found very amusing. And he liked to rile her with his guitar playing and singing. He was especially gifted at whipping up songs on the spur of the moment if he was inspired. Or lying motionless on the couch for days at a time if he wasn't.

He started plucking a light calypso rhythm.

"Once dere was a boy named Eric
Eric, Eric, Er-ic,
His mommy was a former cleric
Eric, Eric, Er-ic,
Mommy brought Eric to the church on Sunday
Eric, Eric, Er-ic
Den Eric he stabbed fifty people on Monday
Eric, Eric, Er-ic."

"That's enough, Duane," she yelled, actually reaching to cover my ears, even though I was already laughing. "Your brother is *not* a maniac, he's just a little tense. And *you're* not helping him any."

Yes he is, I thought, but I couldn't say it. I don't know why, but once again I just couldn't pull the trigger on words. Duane could, though.

"Yes I am," he said. "What this boy needs is poetry to free his soul, not any crappy, phony old *community*."

"'Poetry is devil's wine'—St. Augustine," she said with a triumphant grin.

"Then 'Let's all get stoned'—Brother Ray Charles," he sang, with the unfair advantage of accompanying himself on the guitar.

Sometimes I enjoyed this, the way the two of them would do battle over possession of me. But it occurred to me after a while that it wasn't all that flattering since they seemed to relish the battle whether I stuck around or not. The battle was the thing. So I slithered off to my room, leaving them to it. "We're not finished with this, Eric," she called as I walked away. But she didn't tell me to come back.

I fed my fish, then I fed my Chinese water dragon. She likes mice. Pinky rats, when I can get them, babies, before they have any hair on them yet. They look kind of cute, pink and curled up very

babylike with their eyes closed. Mary, my dragon,
goes crazy for them.

Mary lives in my room in a twenty-nine-gallon
fish tank. A vivarium. She used to have a couple of
roommates, a chuckwalla and a skink. But she ate
them. It's hard to fairly describe how Mary eats mice
so that someone could appreciate it, but it is fascinat-
ing. First she chases the mouse around snapping at it,
trying to get an angle on it so she can grab the head.
Then she seizes the head—her jaws are like a mini
bear trap—and chews on it. It sounds like crunching
the old maids at the bottom of popcorn.   ·

If the mouse's feet keep moving, which happens
much of the time, Mary whips him back and forth,
smashing him on the glass, her cinder block, anything
hard. Then when he stops kicking, she swallows him
whole, the tail sticking out of her mouth like an after-
dinner smoke or a toothpick. I've seen this now a
hundred times, and I can't take my eyes off it. Ever. I
know it's rough stuff. I know just from the faces of
people I used to try to tell it to, when I used to
bother. But people would watch it if it was on *Survival*
or *National Geographic*. I just have it in my room.

The part I don't tell people about is that I have to
help Mary sometimes. She's fat now, and maybe old—
it's hard to tell. But more often than not she can't
catch a full-grown mouse. She'll just lunge at him for

hours, the mouse quivering like he's going to have a heart attack as he hides in the corners. So what I have to do is, I reach in with my ruler and bop the mouse on the head, scrambling his brains. While he convulses on the ground, Mary comes by and scoops him up. Only Mary and I know I do that.

TRADITION

DEATH HAS ALWAYS BROUGHT my family to life more than life itself ever has. My mother, for instance, who most days won't even answer the phone, will spend all day making calls to be the first to spread the news of somebody's croaking or picking up some creepy disease. Not that it made any sense. Nobody around here ever seemed to like another individual, really *like* them, until that individual died. Every dead person who had ever said hello to us was more important than anyone with a beating heart.

My grandmother was one of those. My father's mother. I never knew that anybody liked her at all, until she died. In the days when she was strong enough to visit us, my mother would have to hide the dirty laundry in the cellar and Lysol every floor because she was so afraid of Gram's abuse. *Worthless* was a word my grandmother used on my mother in front of everybody. And my father wouldn't say a word about it, though Ma looked at him with her roundest, wounded-cat eyes. By the time Gram left, usually after about a week, my mother had a bald spot behind each ear the size of a ravioli and flakes of skin powdering her square shoulders. From scratching. And she just turned red with rage, wouldn't speak, whenever Dad got in the same room with her.

"Do you know what she did to me?" Ma stammered after slamming down the phone on their last conversation. "She said I stole her nightgowns, and her money, and her pills. She said the reason my husband was forced to sleep with prostitutes all these years was that I was a big fat porcupine."

"Dad . . . ?"

"Well, of course he didn't. She's a madwoman," she said. "But that's not the point. She's a mean, hateful, demented woman."

But all that was when she was alive.

"I can't believe I was just talking with her three days ago," Ma said as someone squeezed her hand at the funeral home. "She was a *rock*, that woman." The listener, if you could call her that since she was deaf as a stop sign, nodded, smiled, while some young guy held her up by the elbow.

That's pretty much how it went, my mother saying nice things about Gram, Dad liking everybody who came, squeezing hands, kissing cheeks, and directing everyone to go up and grab a peek at the top half of his dead mother. It was a good thing I was only there for window dressing, in my little gangster suit with the wide-spaced pinstripes. Because I just didn't get it. Couldn't see it, couldn't feel it, couldn't join in.

I thought it was over when all the guests had had their shot, and I was ready to move on. Then, starting with my mother, the receiving line that was us—my immediate family, minus Duane, plus some third cousin types—started coming up, back to front. Curling its way toward the casket like a lizard swallowing its own tail, the line became the mourners. My mother passed, hugged my father hard. "I could cry," she said, but didn't *do*.

I hesitated when it was my turn. "I hadn't planned . . ." I whispered to my father. He pulled at my arm and guided me toward the little altar.

Even now she looked mean. They had her pretty well powdered up, whiter than white, like she always looked. But they added some pink to her cheeks, just a small bloom of spring on each side that was shaded into the whiteness gradually enough to look almost natural, except for the fact that color of any kind was not natural to her. Her hairline seemed to have moved back an inch or so since she died, making her temples look squarer than usual. The tiniest smile was planted on her face, which—I won't even talk about how ridiculous that looked on her. In her hands, along with the rosary beads that were twisting like a snake in and out between her bony bent fingers, was a picture of her husband. It was the laminated funeral picture she kept taped to the inside of her cupboard, the only evidence I had that the man existed since she never mentioned him one single time as long as I knew her.

I looked back up at her face. I'd been to these things before, for relatives, friends of my parents', neighborhood people we hardly knew. The thing I noticed mostly at those was that the person dead in the box didn't look a whole lot like the person live on the street. But that wasn't the case here. Gram looked like herself, like she toddled on down to the funeral home under her own power, "Askin' nothin' from nobody," as she always said, then just lay down in the box when she got here.

Dad walked slowly to the sprawling altar of the old church. He had to say a few words at the funeral, and as he neared the twenty-foot wooden statue of God that stood open armed at the head of the church, he looked tinier and tinier. There were about fifty people in the church that was big enough to hold three thousand.

God looked like a gigantic defensive tackle about to pounce on Dad from behind. Dad, in his black suit, with his voice bouncing all around the hollow stone building, hardly seemed like the quarterback. He looked and sounded far away, weak, unsure. You'd think he didn't even know the person he was speaking about, that they just pulled him in off the street to do this because he had the best suit and a P.R. guy's way of being able to talk even though he has nothing much to say.

"And now I know my pa is a happy man," he said, maybe the third time I'd ever heard him mention his father. "He was a patient man, my father, and now he has his reward. Unfortunately, Ma, we here had to give you up for that to be. But you left us plenty. You taught us to stand on our own two feet. You taught us quiet dignity. By example more than words, you taught us—no complaints, no regrets. You told me, 'You're tough, you can take it,' over and over until finally it was true. Thank you."

I heard the sniffles all around. Mainly from people who didn't know Gram well. Ma put her hand around my shoulders and squeezed, like one or both of us was being brave. Dad paused for a long time. At first I thought it was his public relations pause, for effect, when he wants his audience to roll around in his words. Then, though, when he went to start up again, nothing came out. Just a little croak. He cleared his throat. Excused himself. He began again, and it happened again. So for a full minute he stood there silently. His palms planted flat on the lectern, his shoulders up by his ears, he stared out into the crowd, daring anyone to say anything. All was frozen. Not numb, but cold, uncomfortable. I looked up at Ma, who smiled at him in the distance. The brave smile. She didn't get it, didn't see that something *real* was actually happening with Dad.

"But I don't know," he finally said, his voice not loud, but bigger than before, a crack in the quiet. "I don't know if I can tell you all what I'm really thinking. I don't know if my mother would approve. I mean, would I be letting my mother down if I told you all how *alone* I feel right now?"

Once again, he stopped. Waiting for some kind of answer, it seemed. There was a lot of coughing and shifting, but not a word. I looked at Ma. Dad may not have let *his* mother down, but mine looked like her husband had just dropped his pants and mooned the congregation.

The time gave him a chance to listen, to hear his own words echoing around his head. I felt my mouth hanging open like a baby bird waiting to be fed. For once, by accident, Dad had deviated from the script, and I was rooting for him.

When it sank in, he stepped back, cleared his throat, and wiped his brow. Like snapping out of a trance, he straightened up. "Thank you all for coming," he said in his stranger-off-the-street voice, and marched back to our pew.

Irish wake. As much as I know about death and rituals, I still don't know exactly what that's supposed to mean. Everybody has wakes, not just the Irish. There's a dead person, a bunch of live people, and a gathering at somebody's home. I don't know exactly what it is that's supposed to separate the Irish version from any other. Could be the dead person propped up in the middle of the party with a drink in his hand. But I don't think anyone really does that anymore. I could buy it if there was something truly different about it, like a fish wake. A fish in the tank, he's swimming along one minute and no other fish bothers him. Next minute he's dead, and all his buddies turn around and eat all the flesh right off his bones. They respect him right up until the instant of death, but then it's "Well, it's been nice, but . . ." The opposite of the people I know. Fish I think I understand.

Duane was in the living room watching TV when we came in. He'd said sorry but he had no use for any of the religious aspect of the death scene, but he would stay home and get ready for the party. "Let the dead bury their dead" was how he put it, even though Ma has begged him not to quote the Bible.

"You don't own a suit?" Dad said, more disappointed than angry. Duane had on his usual red jeans, like it was any day. He didn't even try to answer, and Dad didn't wait for him to.

But Duane *had* put out a nice spread. Ice bucket, Waterford glasses, decanted wine, plastic trash barrel full of beer. Three kinds of bread, dijon mustard, and eight different cold cuts, including that bologna with the fat globules in it that Gram liked.

"What'd you get *that* for?" I asked. "Nobody's going to eat that."

He smiled. "When the rest of the carcass is gone, I want that little stack of thick-sliced mortadella to stand, my little memorial to Gram."

Ma looked impressed, even proud and happy. "This is very nice, Duane. You did a fine job."

Dad walked in, looked the table over, stuck a rolled piece of boiled ham in his mouth. "If you don't have any more respect than to stand around looking like a harlequin, Duane, maybe you don't need to be here," he said quietly, trying not to make a big deal. He poured himself three fingers of Paddy Irish whiskey, which I'd never seen him drink.

Again, Duane smiled. To Ma and Dad, I'm sure it looked like he was being smartass because he *is* kind of a smartass a lot of the time. But I saw it different. To me it looked less like a grin and more like a wounded animal, flashing all teeth.

"I got respect," he said. "I got more respect than I know what to do with. Respect is the planet I live on. But you can't reach me there, because you don't speak the language."

Whenever he talks like one of the songs he writes, my mother gets a stupefied look and Dad gets flushed, looks somehow humiliated. Duane reached deep in the trash bucket and pulled out a beer, looking right at both of them while he did it. They didn't make a sound as he walked off to his room and slammed the door.

By the time Duane poked his face back out twenty minutes later, the house had filled and divided. In the kitchen sat the wives and mothers and daughters, sipping tea and munching blueberry scones. Everyone listened politely as once again Ma told the story about how Gram always made the girls give up their seats when the men came into a room. "Strong, deeply traditional household"—she nodded—"masons, who hauled brick all day until they couldn't stand up straight without the lubrication of a pint—or six."

The dining room, where the men huddled, was practically silent but for the tinkling of ice in glasses.

Duane straddled the threshold between the two rooms, while everyone tried to pretend he wasn't there. Eventually he just shook his head, dropped off his empty Harp bottle, and took another. "Tradition," he muttered as he walked away. "That's what makes this family great."

Without Duane there to make everybody nervous, the buffet was going down nicely, and just like he figured, the mortadella seemed to be rising like a silo as the rest of the food disappeared. The beer, the wine, the many whiskeys all flowed. I just sat on a bar stool in one corner of the dining room, listening, eating smoked turkey. Dad was buckling under the weight of Paddy, Jameson, and Bushmill's.

I'd never seen him do this. He was getting fuzzy, and talking. As if everything was important to him all of a sudden. But especially family, roots, the auld sod, and banshees.

"I hear their song," he said. "The pipes, the pipes are calling me. I'm going back someday, and won't be returning to this bastard land, I'll tell you."

I wasn't sure what he was talking about, but I liked it. Because he seemed to care. He wasn't much for talking about songs, or pipes calling, or anything, really, that sprang from his own heart rather than some client's list of objectives. His face was ruddy with passion or liquor as the men started moving off,

to join their wives in the kitchen, or to leave the
house altogether to rejoin the 1990s. As they moved
away, I wanted more than ever to move closer. So I
did.

"Dad?" I said cautiously.

"Mornin', boyo," he said. He pulled me close and
we sat side by side.

I wanted to talk, so badly did I want to talk, but I
didn't know what I wanted to say. Yes I did. I wanted
to say great job, Dad. At the church, great job, and
right here, right now, great job, Dad. I like what you
said. I don't suppose most of the people there exactly
know what you said, but it felt like a whole lot of
something to me.

That's what I *wanted* to say. But it was impossible.
It occurred to me that I flatly did not know how to
talk such talk. To talk real. I didn't have the equipment, just like everybody else in my family. Except,
all of a sudden, for Dad. He was *drinking* the equipment.

So instead of trying to talk, I sat under his wing as
he held me and talked about his mother and father,
his childhood, the old country, and the banshee softly
calling him back there. It was close to a dream, this
almost closeness with my father. I felt something because I *wanted* to feel something, we shared something because we badly *wanted* to share, to value

something, anything, together, to *connect*. By the time
we heard the music, I felt we were someplace, somebody, we hadn't been before.

Softly, as if it was coming from the next yard, or
the roof, the guitar started ringing. Duane's guitar, to
be sure, but not his usual metal-picking harshness. It
sounded softer, even, than if he was playing with his
fingertips alone. Like wind brushing across the
strings, "Tura Lura Lural" floated into the room.

The man helping his wife with her coat stopped.
The middle-aged woman walking out the door came
back in. The conversations winding down in the
kitchen halted, as everyone turned an ear to Duane's
room at the far end of the hall. It didn't even sound
like guitar as much as it did like harp. That's his gift,
Duane. He can make his instrument sound like a
garbage truck or a baby's cry or a flute if he wants to.

It was like one of those dream sequences in a
movie. Everyone in the house either stopped cold or
slowed way down to where it looked like we were all
kind of dangling above the floor. Ma and the ladies
drifted in from the kitchen, Dad stopped drinking.
All faces first stared down the hall toward the music,
then up toward the ceiling, relaxing, appreciating, almost praying.

From "Tura Lura" Duane eased into "Danny
Boy," so smoothly you would almost have thought

it was the same song. Everyone swayed, but very slightly. Two women behind Ma, when I sneaked a peek, had tears bubbling down their faces onto their black dresses. Ma herself was looking stunned, inspired, proud. But no tears.

"It's too bad he went sour," the husband whispered as he finally dropped his wife's coat over her shoulders. "He was so gifted."

Still, you could not hear a single pick stroke, like Duane was making the strings sing with his brain alone. "Danny Boy," with the pipes calling, glen to glen, gave way to an "Amazing Grace" that sounded as full, as busy, yet as gentle as a band of bagpipes breathing its way through each room, kissing every mourning forehead.

He could have gone on like that for hours, so hypnotized were his listeners. I know that *I* couldn't have moved if I wanted to. Which I didn't. But suddenly his door opened. He must have done it with his foot, because his playing didn't hesitate. Everyone stared, like Our Lady of Fatima herself was coming down that hall. Though when they saw him, the spell was broken. All the guests headed for the coats, even the ones who usually stay until you start emptying ashtrays and wrapping the food in foil. It was Duane's face that did it. You couldn't see it, his face. The guitar was covering it, and his tiny portable amplifier was hanging from his belt. He was playing all that music, that angelic music, that spiritual music, that Irish music, with his tongue.

I turned immediately to see my mother's reaction. She had spun back into the kitchen, wordlessly brushing by her guests. Dad practically hurdled the dining-room table to get back to the bar, bury his face, and pretend that Duane didn't exist. Pretend that he and everyone else hadn't just been taken to where no church had ever brought them, spiritwise, by sour old Duane, his ax, and his tongue.

I stayed on my bar stool, turned back toward Duane. The house was already cleared of guests, like they'd all just witnessed one of those foul family secrets nobody should see. After a couple of last tongue sweeps, Duane finished his song. He stood right over me, looked at Dad's back, then back down at me. He laughed, then hopped up on the sideboard against the wall, his hips nestled between a tall crystal decanter of red wine and a bottle of Irish Mist. Taking up an empty beer bottle and kicking his feet as they dangled two feet above the floor, he started playing again. Instead of fingering the chords, he took the bottle and maneuvered it up and down the neck of the guitar, making the instrument sing, whine, little low screams that sounded so much like that sound. That painful sound. That foreign sound. That sound nobody in this house wanted to hear. Duane's playing sounded just like a human voice wailing.

Dad drank. And poured. And drank again. Ma stormed out of the kitchen hiding her face as she beat it for the bedroom. Duane smiled, but only for a second; then he winced like he was carrying a load of cinder blocks for the old stonemasons. Or like he was cutting himself with a knife.

I couldn't stop watching Duane. He was so beautiful, so right. Where he never quite seemed to fit anywhere, doing anything anybody else did, my brother at this moment looked like God built him for nothing else but to sit between booze bottles on a sideboard and play. And that's why he was beautiful. He knew it, knew who he was.

Finally Dad left too. Duane wailed on. No song in particular, although I did hear pieces of "Bye, Bye Love," by the Everly Brothers and "Summer Wind" by Frank Sinatra, which Gram loved ("I lost you/Lost you to the Summer Wind"). She was always crazy for songs about somebody losing something, even though she never seemed to have anything herself. But mostly Duane just played cries.

"Can I clear a room, or what?" Duane said, laughing. He hopped off the sideboard and walked to the beer barrel. Sticking both hands way down deep in the ice, he pulled out two brown bottles and stuck one in my hand.

"I probably shouldn't," I told him, pointing it back at him.

"I guarantee you they won't say a thing. I guaran-*tee*," he said. "Have a drink with me and Gram, won't you?"

I got all shaky, and my stomach buzzed. There was so much stuff swirling around me now—feeling sad for Gram, nervous and excited about sort of daring my parents the way Duane does, and wanting to be together with him like this—that I couldn't get a good handle on any of it. I cracked the beer open.

Duane clinked his bottle against mine. "Good-bye, leather face," he said. "We'll miss you. Not a whole hell of a lot, but we'll miss you."

"Duane!" I almost spat my first swallow.

"She wouldn't mind, Eric. She was tough. You have to remember who you're toasting, here." He picked up a disk of mortadella, offered it up like the host at mass, and popped the whole thing in his mouth.

RAW AND REAL

BY THE NEXT MORNING it was all gone. Gone with the imaginary stains Ma was washing from perfectly clean, unused saucers, the way nutty people scrub their hands, over and over and over. Gone with the crumbs Dad was scooping off the rug to dump into the garbage disposal, only to make the thing whine like a cat with nothing but crumbs to chew. Gone, of course, with the bar setup, which Ma broke down and stored away first thing in the morning.

Dad was already dressed in his sharp suit for work, but he looked like a little mole, snuffling around the floor on his elbows and knees cleaning up. The blood had to be pounding in his head, the way his face was all flushed. I got down and started helping him.

He looked right up into my face. At first like he didn't quite know me, but then like he was grateful.

Silently we ferreted out every crumb from around the table legs and under every chair. Then we stood up, each with his little bounty cupped in one hand. Dad wavered a bit when he got completely upright. And he winced.

"Does it hurt, Dad?" I said.

He spun away from me and headed toward the kitchen. "Does what hurt?"

"I don't know, your head? Or something? From yesterday?"

"Why should he be hurt?" Ma said as we neared her. She was drying her hands on a dish towel, and her forehead was striped with furrows. "There's nothing wrong with your father." When she stopped drying, she folded her arms across her chest.

I turned to Dad as we both dumped our crumbs into the sink. He looked at me with a small, happy, pained smile, like he was glad I asked anyway. "I'm fine, son," he said.

We sat at the newly clean table and Ma got us some breakfast. Toast, eggs, cereal, but none of the many rolls or muffins left over from yesterday. Even though we have nothing against leftovers. Those were in the trash.

Ma put a hot plate of eggs in front of Duane's spot, as if she could sense him coming.

"Hey y'all," Duane said, food in his mouth before

he even hit the chair. "Hey Dad, how's the old melon this morning?"

Ma stabbed her head in from the kitchen. Dad didn't look up from the newspaper. "I'm fine," he said. "There is not a thing wrong with your father," she said.

Duane was prepared. I think if they'd answered any other way, he'd have been disappointed. He started singing, halfway between a rap and something from *Camelot*.

> *"No brain, no pain*
> *Yesterday's passed*
> *But we're the same*
> *Don't look at the pain*
> *Pain is shame*
> *Don't listen to Duane*
> *Duane's insane*
> *No pain, no gain*
> *No Duane*
> *No pain*
> *No shame*
> *No gain"*

He looked all around the room and smiled broadly. Like my parents were going to say "Hey, way to go, Duane."

"Duane, if you're on narcotics, I want you to tell us so we can get you help," Ma said. She knew he didn't do drugs. She just wished it was something that easy to understand. Dad just nodded, folded his paper, and left. As much as Duane's guitar bothers them, it seems to be his a capella work that drives them into the street. The tires screeched in the driveway.

"Nice song, D," I said as I got up to go. Even though he lost me right about the "Duane's insane" part.

I really intended, when I left the house, to go to school. But each step I took in that direction was heavier and slower than the last. I just wasn't finished with yesterday yet, is what it was.

Where I went to was where I always go when I am so sick and sorry and dead inside from feeling nothing and seeing nothing and getting nothing from the people around me that I'd lick the tears off a baby's face just to steal a taste of somebody's real inside self. Where I went, after all that, was the funeral home.

I like to be near dead things. Dead *people*. I don't know what it's all about, but I know it's different from my family's "dead folks—don't ya just love 'em" phoniness. It is different. It's not like them. For one thing, I kind of prefer that the dead bodies I'm near didn't belong to people I knew. For another, I like to get up close, to lay a finger on them if I get a chance, to get involved with them. This, I know, would not interest my parents.

I'm not crazy; I'm aware that this thing I have puts me somewhere outside the mainstream of civilization. But just barely outside, I think. *American Heritage* ran an article last month on how people in the 1800s used to take pictures of their kids when they were dead. They'd open their eyes—who was the lucky family member who got to peel the eyelids back?—prop them up with a favorite toy, surround them with friends and family, and snap away. There was one picture of twins. One had died, the other hadn't. Eight-year-olds arm in arm, in their adorable sailor suits, identical, until you noticed one of them listing to the side with some kind of fluid running out of his ear. And the live kid was smiling.

Gormely's funeral home lies on my route where I run. Inside Gormely's is one of the better live guys around, named McLaughlin. Mortician's assistant is what he calls himself, which means he does all the grunt work around the place, then makes himself scarce when it's time for the slick funeral-director types to slide on their suits and make grieving families feel better with the warmth they learned at the New England Institute of Mortuary Sciences near Fenway Park. I have one of their NEIMS sweatshirts.

The first time I met McLaughlin was at the cemetery. I was just running through, but he was working himself dizzy, trying all by himself to right about 150 headstones that were toppled for the hundredth time by some kids my age who had a more normal sense of community than I've got. I stopped to try and help him, but each stone weighed about seven tons. He wouldn't stop, though. His spine is bent anyway from being six foot three and sixty-one years old—sixty-one devilish hard ones to boot, he said—but as he went from stone to stone wrapping his whole wiry self around it and pulling, he looked like a fishing rod with a marlin on the line. We stayed in that cemetery for two hours, McLaughlin getting more desperate with every failure, until we found the stone we could budge. A plain white one, cement instead of granite, one third the thickness of all the others, a poor person's slab that said nothing on it but the name, Rigby.

We sweated, drooling like farm beasts, until finally me and McLaughlin got the thing upright. I stood up, my own back aching now. McLaughlin then uprighted himself, as much as he could. He stared down at what we'd done, reached slowly into his pocket and pulled out a red handkerchief. He mopped his deeply lined, honest forehead, then his eyes as tears started to roll. Neither of us had said a word till then.

"Is it such a big deal, really?" I said tentatively, since I didn't know anything about this nutty guy after all.

He didn't even look at me, stared instead at Rigby. "These is *people*," he sighed.

McLaughlin decided then that I was people too. Which is a pretty big deal, because there aren't many live people who McLaughlin feels is *people*. "A lifetime of dealing with our species has taught me to appreciate that the quiet ones is the best of 'em," he said when I took him up on his invitation to come see him at the funeral home. He was receiving a shipment of caskets. Something about it was thrilling to me, being there when they arrived early one morning, just the truck driver, McLaughlin, and me. And the big shining mahogany boxes that in a few hours would be filled with dead. Bones without motors. Flesh without blood.

"Can I go look around inside?" I asked.

"Sure," he laughed. "Just so long as you don't bugger no corpses while you're in there."

"Jesus, you have one gross imagination," I said.

"Think I'm lying?" McLaughlin said casually as he signed the receipt. "People offer me *money* to pimp for the dead folks I got. Some sick sonbitches out there."

That morning I went directly to Gormely's. I

walked around back to the service entrance like always, but he wasn't there. So I sat on the step to wait. A few seconds later the bulkhead leading to the cellar popped open, and out came McLaughlin wheeling a barrow full of dead flowers up the ramp. He went right past me, delivering the flowers to the far end of the small parking lot, around the garage where they hold the caskets. There he dumped the flowers in a pile, next to where Mr. Gormely has his compost heap and tomato plants.

When he came back my way, McLaughlin stopped and dumped the wheelbarrow in front of me. Giving me the usual expression of no-smile, no-frown, he motioned me to follow him, then put his long finger to his lips. "Shh" was the whole conversation.

I followed him into the cellar, then up the back stairs. It was a big old Victorian house, with servants' quarters, large kitchen, mud room by the back door, all on the back side of the house—McLaughlin territory. We walked up to the second floor, along the stairs that were half steps, half very steep handicapped ramp, where McLaughlin had to push readied bodies up to the upstairs viewing rooms.

When we reached the second floor, we were in what looked like a mini teachers' lounge, or a factory break room. One long table, a sink, a small refrigerator, and a coffee maker in a wood-paneled 10 x 12

room. I just looked at McLaughlin. He didn't look at
me. Instead he walked directly to the wall opposite
the door and pressed his face against it for a long
time. When he was done, he waved me over. What he
had his eye to was a wide seam in the paneling. I
looked through it to find that it corresponded to an
open seam on the other side, peeking out through
some drapes. I pulled back when I saw somebody
move in the other room, and looked to McLaughlin.
Silently, he directed me to keep looking.

It was a prefuneral service. The folding chairs
were all lined up in a block like a small chapel. A
woman in her twenties, not very nice to look at, sat
in the front row staring blankly ahead, staring right at
me, it appeared. Behind her sat three old men in
army uniforms—the kind of uniforms you only see in
movies anymore, with the little Boy Scout–style hats.
One of them looked only at his hands in his lap, the
second only at the back of the woman's long black
hair, and the last had his eyes closed. Besides the two
pin-stripe-suited parlor employees stationed at the
door behind everybody, trying to make each other
laugh with stupid faces, there was nobody there but a
bunch of empty chairs.

It only then occurred to me that the center of attention, the point of it all, the dead man, was literally
right under my nose. I looked down and there he was,

in my face. At first he looked gigantic and heavily mapped, like a parade float head, the way things look when you spy them through a hole. But when I got him in focus, I saw that he was in fact a tiny little old guy. He wore the same outfit as his friends, but the hat looked borrowed, way too big and not smartly angled to one side like the others'. His forehead was something, though. Long, deeply cut furrows spread like sound waves emanating from his nose, in that wavy V shape artists use to put sea gulls in ocean paintings. The cuffs of his pressed green jacket stretched way down over his fingers, the fingers being the only evidence that they actually put his body inside the suit instead of cutting off his head and setting it on top.

Everybody just sat there, not doing anything, but looking like they were content with that. The NEIMS grads, though, were looking bored, checking their watches. Finally, somebody new arrived. In the same uniform, even older than all the rest, he shuffled through the doorway with . . . bagpipes slung over his shoulder. The man walked up to one of the attendants, who at first shook his head no repeatedly. When the old man persisted, the second attendant joined in; then both shrugged their shoulders. As the soldier approached the casket, they closed the big double doors to keep the sound in.

Making those random, competing, multiple sounds that make one set of bagpipes sound like a whole orchestra tuning up, the man started. Squeals, sighs, squeaks, and cries pulled together out of the noise, and in a few seconds he was blowing "America the Beautiful" at a pace so slow and sad as to stop your heartbeat.

The woman in front buried her face in her hands, her elbows propped on her knees. The middle of the three soldiers—the youngest-looking at ninety or so—put his arms around his buddies. The one with his eyes closed still didn't open them, but leaned close and put his tired head on his friend's shoulder. The player, the bagpipe man, was turning deep pink in the face, the only real color in the room, until he finally let the song trail off, not like a real ending, but like the tide going out.

When the song finished, the three in the second row stood and saluted. The bagpipe soldier pushed his instrument around to the back, reached over—like he was reaching for me—and straightened his comrade's hat. Then he saluted and walked away. The attendants opened the doors for him, nothing funny left on their faces.

McLaughlin's hands were on my shoulders. I turned to look at him and saw there, in his calm, worn face, that he knew exactly. Like a ghoul, he fed on it. Like a vampire sucking the life, the blood, he found that this was where to find it, the place where people *said* they were sad, they were hurt, said they didn't want to be alone. Where people let it rip and didn't give a damn who knew about it. I saw—and stole—more emotion raw and real in that room in twenty minutes than I'd gotten from my family in fourteen years. And McLaughlin knew.

He took a sip from a cup of coffee he'd made while I was tranced, then brought the cup down to reveal the tiniest, briefest smile.

"My home," he said. "It ain't like your home, is it?"

WISH YOU
WERE HERE

I COULDN'T GET ENOUGH of it then. After the World War I guy's service I had to get to the cemetery to see him laid to rest. I hit the street running, headed straight for the cemetery down the street where just about everybody from Gormely's gets buried. When I blew through the iron gate, it occurred to me that I had no clue where in the big field of graves they'd be putting the guy. So I loitered near the entrance, hoping to catch the people I'd seen through the crack on their way by.

I waited three quarters of an hour. Nobody came through. Could have gone somewhere else, I thought. But that wasn't it. He wasn't buried at all. "Put a match to the old duffer" was how McLaughlin put it later on.

But I was there, and I was wanting. So I went looking.

Midweek you've got the dead folks pretty much

to yourself, except for the odd funeral, since nobody really comes out visiting but for holidays and Sundays. Except for old people, who I think like to visit their late friends as much as their current ones. But they might as well be ghosts themselves the way they float through here, so quiet, so spacey, like you could pass right through them if they got in your way.

So I cruised around looking for I don't know what. Looking I suppose for a funeral that had nothing to do with me so I could peep in again at how real people do it, how they give themselves up. So I could feel what they feel, if only for a few minutes, if they'd only show me how. Looking to do my ghoul thing, snack on somebody else's feelings till I'm all full up and can return to the world of the living dead until I need my next hit.

White was what I saw. When the sun beats on a sea of headstones like it was that day, there's no more bleached-out spot on earth. Not like in the movies, where there's always a misty rain at a gravesite. Every stone looked white, the black ones just a little less white, and neat and square and aligned to the millimeter. It was soothing, the blankness, the quiet, the steady, soft pat-patting of my Sauconys up and down the hilly, winding road. But I didn't come to be soothed. And after a while the clean gentleness began to grate.

Until I came across the fresh one. It was in the

third large square section I passed through. They'd just finished digging a new grave and left it sitting there, open. I walked right up to it, a little thrill in my chest from the ridiculous thought that I'd maybe find a corpse just sort of dumped inside. It was empty, except for a shovel standing up at one corner of the perfectly cut rectangular hole, another lying on the ground above. I walked right up to the edge, letting the toes of my shoes hang out over, the way some people just have to do when they're standing on a rooftop.

I took the smell in deep. The smell of wet dirt. Of the always freshly cut lawn of the grounds. Of whatever it is they use on their soil to make the grass so velvety, now filling the air with all those shovelfuls of dirt overturned and overturned into the heap beside me. I closed my eyes, held my hands by my sides, and breathed it in.

I jumped in. I stood for a minute with my arms outstretched touching both side walls. I took the little walk down one end, touched the end wall, the earth wetter down there for some reason, then back up to put both palms flat on the fourth. There were others down here, on four sides. Neighbors. Maybe with their hands pressed against the wall just opposite mine, breathing up all this fine dirt. The smell surrounded me, as thick as if it were coming right out of me, this smell of moss and mold and minerals. It couldn't have been heavier if I'd been buried alive right here.

I lay down. Toes pointed first up at the sky, then ballet straight as my whole body tensed with the excitement of it. My hands opened and closed, opened and closed at my sides. I forced my eyes shut; they sprang open again like window shades. I breathed slowly, rhythmically, the way I do it when I run, and began to calm. My eyes drew closed with no effort. Hands and feet went limp. The clamminess of the dirt on the back of my head and seeping through my shirt, at first chilling, was now an embrace.

My eyes shot open. I looked up into the sky, all along the precise edges of the grave. Something had stirred, something was disturbed, although there was no bush to rustle, no leaves, no gravel to crunch. It just seemed. Someone's eyes had been on me.

Or I was just too wired. Besides, I didn't care. They're gone, if there even was anybody. Hope they thought I was a dead person and ran. I just wanted my peace anyway. I closed my eyes, wiggled my fingers loose. Stay shut, dammit. I breathed, slowly, deeply.

It was gone. I stood, climbed up the shovel handle. When I poked my head up above ground, I propped myself on my elbows, the rest of me still hanging below. I looked in all directions. There was nobody anywhere. Good thing. If there was, I'd have taken that spade to his head, for chasing it away.

I didn't go to school, but I did go to hockey practice. Never even thought about skipping it, because that's what I do. I'm a hockey player. I go to practice every day the same way I brush my teeth, sleep, or take meals—without thinking about it. But as I walked home, I was thinking about it. Because I was hurting. My hips hurt, my knuckles hurt, my knees hurt, my shoulders hurt. All because of the way I played that day. I hit everything that moved. My own team, after all, and I flew all over the ice, crashing into anyone bold enough to lay a stick on the puck, which, by the end of the day, was nobody. Coach even called it quits a little early because of how embarrassing it got, guys just letting the puck lie there rather than risk playing with me. But I didn't hear a word about it. Even the coach didn't want to screw with me.

I only pieced it together, though, on the way home. When the all-over aches gnawed at me and woke me up.

My parents were sitting in the living room when I came in. On the same couch, with only about two feet or so of space between them, which was a pretty big deal.

"Is this the type of thing I should have to hear?" Ma said.

"No, Ma," I sighed. "I guess it isn't." I had no clue what she was talking about, but I didn't care.

"Father Henry said he thought you were a dead person when he saw you. Almost caused him to take a heart attack himself. Lying in a *grave*? Eric."

It was the priest. I *knew* somebody'd been there. "Why didn't Father Henry say anything when he saw me, instead of sneaking around like that?"

"He didn't want to start any trouble," Dad kicked in. Of course Dad would have to defend that motive. Dad's a "let's not start any trouble" kind of guy.

"But he did, though, didn't he?" I said, emboldened now by my visit to the netherworld. "I mean, he told *you*." I thought about it for a second and a smile peeled across my face. "He didn't talk to me because . . . he was *afraid* to talk to me, is that it?"

"Score one for the ghoul," Duane said as he strolled in. He was munching on an ungodly huge turkey leg. He waved it at me. "Want some?" he said as he dropped into the chair across from my parents. "Or maybe you don't like the leg. If you like, I could go to the kitchen and get you something else, a nice hand, maybe, or a couple of slices of face?"

"Duane," Ma snapped, "this is very serious."

"I believe you're right," Duane said. "For once I

agree with you. This is serious stuff."

"Son," Dad said from somewhere deep in his own personal fog, "this is decidedly antisocial behavior. It's the kind of thing that can get you a reputation, as an eccentric. These things stay with you, you know. They make it hard to, well, to make your way in the world."

"For God's sake, Eric, it's just plain demented, and I want it to stop," Ma said. She spoke nervously, staccato, randomly. "We can't have people phoning in reports of your outrageousness. It's not right. And I need you to start going to school regularly. And you're going to church with me again this week."

From my spot in the doorway I was looking over Duane's shoulder into my parents' faces. I didn't know what to say. "I did go to hockey practice. I hurt almost everybody on my team," I said hopefully.

"Well that's fine, Eric," Dad said. "But it still doesn't explain this public antisocial weirdness. . . ."

Duane turned around in the chair to look at me. He gave me a smile and a wink before standing to face my parents. As he hovered over them from across the coffee table, he threw down the gauntlet, which was the turkey leg.

"People, people, people. You just don't get it. The *point*, that is. You're missing it, as usual. Let's play twenty questions, shall we?" He was animated, pacing in front of them the length of the couch, gesturing like a lawyer or a game-show host, clapping loudly and rubbing his hands together. "You!" He pointed at me. "Why do you play with dead people?"

I was actually going to try to answer when he spun back to Ma. "Too late. You! Why do *you* think the boy plays with dead people?"

"This isn't funny, Duane," she sneered.

"That's right, it isn't," he said. He stood in front of her for several silent seconds, but she wouldn't consider his question.

"You!" He pointed at Dad. "How many live human friends does the boy have?"

"I don't get the point," Dad said.

"Cor-rect!" Duane shouted. "It's the answer to a different question, but a fine, true answer anyway."

"You!" He spun back to me. "Does human flesh really taste like veal?"

I laughed. "Too late!" he said, and turned back to my mother. Her face looked like he was offering her some decayed human flesh. She stood up.

"You are the ill one around here, Duane. Maybe *you* should get some help," she said.

"Okay," Duane said, dropping the act for a second, holding both hands out to her. "Will you help me then?" he said quietly.

"You don't want my help," she said, brushing his

hand aside as she made her way toward me. Duane continued to stand, arms outstretched. Dad stood too. He looked like Duane's stuff hadn't bothered him any—he even cracked a smile when Duane called me Bela, because Dad loves horror movies—but it hadn't made an impression on him either.

"Eric, will you go to school tomorrow?" he said. There was real concern in his voice, but it was a tired, bemused concern. I nodded that I would. "School's the place for you. You'll be okay, son— just . . . hang in there, study, work out . . . you'll be okay."

Ma stopped about four feet short of actually walking up to me. "Let's have no more pranks, Eric," she said. Pranks? Jesus, she sure *had* missed the point. "You'll see. The sense of love, of unity that you'll gradually feel from your visits to the church will exorcise these impulses of yours. It is warm in the embrace of the Holy Spirit and of the body of the church."

She nodded, squinted me one of those "buck up, soldier" smiles, and joined Dad in the exodus down the hall.

"*Embrace*," Duane said to her. "Now *there's* a concept. The Holy Spirit can do it. The body of the church can do it. . . . Wait," he called when he was ignored further. "We haven't finished twenty questions: Is it warmer in the ground than in the home?

How long has he been sleeping around? What does the creature seek? Who's responsible . . . ?"

Their bedroom door closed. Not a slam but a calm, controlled thunk, which I think bothered Duane even more.

"You're right," he called out. "Twenty questions *is* a god-awful sonofabitch of a rotten game, isn't it?"

I still stood in the doorway, like I'd just walked in. I stared at Duane as he picked up his turkey leg, walked over, and sat on the couch. He gave me a big grin and patted the seat cushion next to him. "Come on over here and tell me about it, you goddamn gargoyle." He laughed.

It made me smile back, but I shook my head. "I have to feed Mary and the fish," I said. "And it's been kind of a long day." He nodded and saluted me with his drumstick as he flipped on the TV. He understood what I really meant.

I love my brother. I could never tell him, though.

SECOND
PERIOD

SECOND
PERIOD

Ready, Killer?

THE PLACE I COME CLOSEST to having everything under control is the hockey rink. At hockey I'm a natural, so I'm told.

"Oh god yes," Dad said when I asked if I was as good as Duane was before he went sour. "You're far better than he ever was. Duane was almost as fast and strong and deft with the stick as you are, but he didn't have anything at all resembling the *passion* you have." Dad was into a little public-relations spin control here. Duane was great when he played, so good that the team I'm on won't let anyone wear his old number-88 jersey. And while I am good at hockey, better than most, not as good as some, the *passion* Dad talks about is mostly his own.

It was a spooky thing, the way hockey would completely change my father. Just the mention of it, the approach of some bush-league tournament, the sight of my equipment lying on the living-room floor—that was the only stuff I could leave absolutely anywhere I wanted to—lit him up. He'd pick up my helmet or my protective cup and balance it lightly on his fingertips as he talked happily about something he'd seen me, or Duane, or Wayne Gretzky, do on the ice one time. Sometimes, when he's into one of his bluer funks, he'll barely say a word to any of us for days, not like he's mean, just like he's terribly weary and gone, gone someplace far off inside himself. But put him in a frosted arena with no heat in February in Norway, Maine, while I'm grunting it up for him down on the ice, *then* you see passion.

I'm sure the thing he likes about me more than anything else is that my head—big, broad, blocky, with whitish hair buzzed close—looks a lot like a hockey helmet. He cannot pass me on the way to the bathroom without knocking on my head, or butting me, and laughing. If we're "in season." I play from September to April, and some years he doesn't manage a real smile from May to August.

"Look at you, ol' boy." He always calls me ol' boy when it's sports related. "That hockey equipment is practically redundant. A strapper, is what you are."

A strapper, by the way, is what my father isn't. He's almost six feet tall, but he only weighs about 150 pounds. He always swears that if he drank milk when he was a kid, he'd be playing for the Bruins today. But since he didn't drink his milk, he's in public relations. And *I'm* in hockey.

"You ready, killer?" he whispered in my ear while I lay in bed. It was still puck black, in the early hours of another of the million dead-winter Saturdays. I rolled over to see him a couple of inches from my face, without even his glasses on yet. Smiling like a kid, kind of silly, kind of scary.

"Not exactly *ready*, Dad," I said. "But give me a few minutes."

He rubbed my head hard, shaking me all over the place. "Good man," he said. "You get ready and I'll get on the 'cakes." Pancakes. We always have them, and he always talks like a lumberjack, when we're going to hockey.

This time it was St. Albans, way up there in Vermont. It was a four-hour drive each way, but Dad didn't mind at all. The same way he didn't mind taking me, practically in the middle of the night, to games in Portland, Bar Harbor, Laconia, White River Junction, or Saratoga Springs. The guy would take me to Iceland for a hockey game if I wanted, and sing or whistle the whole way. And the level of his excitement was directly related to how close the game site was to God's Country—O Canada. So St. Albans, just a short scream from Cowansville, Quebec, had him giggly.

"What are you thinking about for today, ol' boy?"

Dad said while searching for one of the hundreds of country music stations floating around north of Boston. "You thinking about potting a few, maybe a hat trick? Or do you think they're going to need you to be hitting more today?"

At first I didn't realize he was talking to me. I thought he was still singing "Whiskey River."

"Huh?" I said. That kind of response bothers most parents—it would make my mother put up the old dukes—but Dad loved it when I talked like a jock.

"Ah, you big mug," he laughed. He hammered the top of my head playfully with his fist. "Go back to sleep." He'd landed on a crackly country station from the White Mountains, started singing, "'Out in the West Texas town of El Paso/I fell in love with a Mexican girl. . . .'"

I watched him. His eyes squinted in a frozen smile under his John Deere cap that he got with our lawn mower, and he steered the Subaru with one finger.

"No, really, Dad. What did you ask me?"

"Eric, I was just asking what was on your mind. What you were thinking about. But it's not important." He pushed the hat back a little, scratching his forehead and revealing more baldness than when his hair is combed.

"Well, I think it's important, what's on my mind," I said. I kept staring at him. He wasn't looking right at me, but he knew.

"Certainly it is, son," he said, but he squirmed in his seat. He pulled the hat back down low and turned the radio down. "Shoot," he said.

"I'm thinking . . . I'm thinking maybe we don't have to talk about hockey right now. I'm thinking we might talk about something else. Like about *your* job, Dad. I'm thinking about public relations. Can you tell me more about it? Do you like it? Is it interesting? How did you wind up in it? Is it something you always wanted to do?"

He didn't say anything. But his look did. He stopped smiling, gave me one short, sideways glare. In a whiff he went from his "On the Road Again" joy face to his trapped-like-a-rat dinner-table face. Like now I'd spoiled the great time we were having. He turned the radio back up and stared at the road ahead. I went back to sleep, which is what I usually do during these long rides.

"Forget the puck," Dad screamed. "Follow your man. Follow through." His voice followed me everywhere on the ice. A couple hundred people at most come to these games, in arenas that can hold five thousand. So his voice can howl, like the Wizard of Oz's.

"Ya, forget the puck," my man said to me as we waited for a face-off. "Just follow me." Even my own team got a charge out of it. "Hey Eric, is your old man here by any chance?" one said.

It became a haunt. Everybody on the St. Albans team took a turn at some point, skating by me and saying, "Forget the puck. Forget the puck." My man, Lanois, had a party. The best player I'd ever faced, Lanois was no more than two years away from playing on one of the Canadian junior teams. He was skating rings around me, dumping the puck to one of his wingers, turning me completely around, then taking the pass back for an easy goal. Four times in the first period he did it. My father was screaming so loud and so fast that it wasn't even words anymore. "Buuug bugaboolug bugaboolug, Eric!" Nobody on my team would look at me, but everyone on the other team did. I was supposed to be the leader.

Then two things came together at once to change things. One, my father stopped yelling at me. *Not* screaming might not seem to be a big event, but when Dad quit, it was like a sonic boom in the hollow arena. Somehow it was more humiliating still.

The second thing, like this was all frozen in a slow-mo game film, was that Lanois smiled at me. He was bearing down on me, one on one, and before laying one of his deke moves on me, he hesitated, grinned through his crisscrossed face mask, then plowed toward me.

It was true that I didn't have it that day. It was also true that Lanois could, even on my better days, fake me right up into the stands with his slickness. But at that moment, with the heat filling my helmet, the heat that comes when the blood fills my ears, the heat that always seems to be there just before I do something . . . at that moment, it just wasn't going to happen. I did what I hadn't been doing all along. I stopped skating backward, dug my blades in, it must have been a half inch into the ice. And when it came time for Lanois to slither past, I blew up, right in his face. Two hands on my stick, I cross-checked that superstar sonofabitch right in the face mask so hard, his skates were above my head when his helmet smacked the ice.

I was numb when the referee ushered me off. Manhandled me, really, which referees aren't supposed to do to kids. But I understood. It was pretty crappy, what I did. But I sure heard a lot of hooting in the stands, one voice above the rest.

I got five minutes in the penalty box, though they should have thrown me out. Lanois was out of it from that point on. First, he was out of it because I'd rung his bell pretty good. But even after he recovered, he wasn't a factor. He just didn't seem to have the charge he had before. And the rest of the team went into the tank with him. I should talk—I didn't score either.

But I didn't have to. We won by something like 10–8.

Usually, victory meant that anything I did during the game was okay. But just before I left the dressing room, Coach put a firm grip on my arm. Very quietly but very seriously, he whispered, "Eric, your next criminal act will be your last as a member of this team. Get it under control."

I was pretty shaken as I walked across the parking lot after that. I guess I just hadn't seen it as savage as Coach did. And neither did Dad.

"*I* wouldn't screw around with you," Dad said as he shoved my gear through the hatchback. "No, boy. I'd stay far, far away from ol' left defense."

"Ya, Dad," I sighed. As he gunned the car out of the parking lot, I slunk way down in the seat. The blade of my stick poked out between the seats, by my ear.

"And I still say those helmets are bad for the sport." He stuck a long, thin cigar in his mouth—the postgame ritual that he never repeats anywhere, anytime else. "Those big helmets with the stupid cages covering the player's entire face, they take the individuality away from the players. And the false sense of security they give, that's what makes the game violent. You wouldn't see all the nasty stickwork that mars the game so much if they didn't wear the helmets." My father wanted my victims to *not* have helmets on.

"I've heard that, Dad," I said. My eyes were closed. "I don't know. . . ." I fell asleep to the sound of French hillbilly tunes, Dad faking French-sounding nonsense lyrics, the smell of the cigar soaking into my clothes. When I woke up, the radio was off. Dad's cap was on the seat between us, his thin, cardboard-brown hair flattened to his skull. His face was all pinched up—his everyday face—and he was driving slowly.

I didn't need to look out the window to know we were nearing home.

Naked

I SAW MY FATHER NAKED this morning. When I walked into the bathroom at about seven o'clock, I found him standing in front of the full-length mirror staring at himself.

"Whoa, sorry, Dad," I said, and stepped back.

He turned his face to me slowly, as if I'd just woken him up. "Huh?" he said, seemingly unaware of his nudity.

"Nothing, Dad."

"Need to get in here?"

I backed farther away. "Nah. I'm all set. I'm sorry I bothered you."

"Don't worry about it, son," he said quietly, and resumed looking at his full-length reflection.

I walked straight to Duane's bedroom. A strange, oddly comforting place, Duane's room, and funny when you match it up with Duane himself. It's covered—bedspread, wallpaper, lamps, rug, and drapes—

with Star Wars *Return of the Jedi* decor. My mother did it up when the movie came out and Duane was just a kid. About fifty times since then she has tried to re-decorate, but Duane refuses to let her. With every year it becomes more ludicrous as Duane grows into a sophomore, junior, now senior in high school, and the movie fades further and further from memory. Duane uses words like kitschy and campy to describe it, but my mother is clearly mortified over it. Both ways, it means big fun for Duane.

He was getting dressed for school. He always goes to school.

"I just saw Dad naked," I blurted.

"Kind of a fright, isn't it?"

"Ya," I said, reassembling it in my brain. "He looks little without his clothes, weak, way too white. And kind of crumpled up."

"That's him all right," Duane said as he stepped up to his own dresser mirror. "Is he in front of the bathroom mirror?"

"Ya," I said, sitting on the end of Duane's bed. "Have you seen this before?"

"Hell yes. He does it just about every morning."

"Has Ma seen it?"

Duane grinned. "Ma's *never* seen him naked. He does it while she's at church." He regarded his reflection. Shaking his head to make his long hair fly all around, he then raised his hands as if he was going to straighten it out. Suddenly he stopped, and from over his shoulder I could see that satisfied look again in the mirror. "Perfect," he said, even though it looked the same as when he rolled out of bed.

"Well what's it all about, Duane? I mean, is he going bizarro on us now?"

Duane turned around and shrugged at me. "Could be, but I don't think so. I think it has more to do with the fact he's going to turn forty in a few weeks. He's having a little spell over it, is my guess. He's driving faster too. Have you heard him leaving patches in the driveway? You know, approaching death, life passing him by, is this all there is, that kind of shit. It'll pass."

I stood up, paced the length of the bed a couple of times, which amused Duane. He always thought it was funny when I was tense. "Well, I don't like it, Duane. I don't like seeing him like that. It's kind of scary."

"Sure, it's not a pretty sight. But if I know one thing in this world, then this is the thing I know: Everybody looks worse with their clothes off."

"Not everybody," I said, hoping.

He put his hands on his hips. "*Every*body."

"Not Little Martha," I begged. Little Martha is his girlfriend, who is nineteen, has a job and a Jeep, and who I adore more than he does.

"Yes," he said, and paused for big dramatic effect. "Even Little Martha."

"Jesus, Duane." I paced harder, grabbing the comforter with the picture of Yoda and clutching it as I went. "Y'know, this brutal honesty stuff of yours can be a real pain in the ass. Sometimes it's like you just don't want to leave me anything to live for."

That made him laugh even harder. He wasn't being mean, he just couldn't resist when I was nerved up. He shook his head. "Eric, you don't know what you want, do you? Everybody either says too little or too much for your liking."

I didn't like that.

He stopped my pacing by grabbing my shoulders.

"Don't do that," I said. "You know I don't like to be touched."

He raised his hands. "Sorry, sorry. Say, I have a treat for you. Little Martha's coming by to give me a ride to school. Wanna come?"

With great effort I managed not to swallow my own tongue.

"That might be nice," I said.

"I'll tell her to keep her clothes on, so you don't kill yourself."

When Ma came in from church, we were at the kitchen table eating cold cereal out of the boxes. I was eating Quaker 100% Natural Cereal, because I'm an athlete. Duane was munching Lucky Charms. "I love the way those little marshmallow things feel all metallic on my teeth," he said. "It starts my day off with a spark."

"Eric? Up and dressed already?" She said it like I was alone at the table.

"It's my influence, Ma," Duane said. "I got him all hot to go to school."

It took her a few seconds to respond, what with all those departures from the script packed into one statement. *Me*, hot for school? *Duane*, an influence for good? This wasn't quite fair to her, right as she was coming in from mass, where she knew all the lines by heart. She sat down at the table with us, which was a surprising-enough response.

"Well," she said tentatively, not quite sure if there was a punchline coming. "This is good. This is very good. I don't know how you did it, Duane, but thank you. You know, you are a very flawed individual, but I have to say you have always had the right attitude about school, and it wouldn't hurt for your brother to emulate you. In this area."

"Thanks, Ma," Duane said, shaking his head and laughing a little.

Then she sat back, still in her gray cloth coat with her rectangular black purse in front of her, she looked back and forth between the two of us, and she smiled.

Duane and I both stopped chewing. This was much more shocking than my father in his birthday suit.

"Yes," she said again, "this is good. This is very good."

By some complete freak, we had made her happy, if only for the moment. But it was a pretty decent-feeling moment.

"Let me make you guys some *real* breakfast," she said, and got herself quickly busy. "And what about your father? Have you seen him? It's getting harder and harder lately to get him out of here in the morning. Is he even dressed yet?"

Duane spat a few blue marshmallow diamonds, green clovers, and yellow stars as he laughed. Ma didn't even notice. "Ya, Ma," he said. "He's rambling around here someplace."

Ma thoroughly enjoyed herself making us bacon, eggs, and French toast. She even sang a little "Ave Maria" while she was at it. Duane was inspired enough to join in, but he sounded like Jerry Lewis. Not even the crying-at-the-telethon Jerry Lewis, which would be bad enough, but the mental-defective Jerry Lewis of the old movies.

"Let's not spoil this, okay, Duane?" Ma said, putting a hand lightly on his shoulder and a plate of food in front of him. He didn't sing anymore.

I finished my food and told Ma how good it was. She was still relatively chirpy as she swept the dirty dishes away. "You know, Ma," I said, not wanting to rain on her parade exactly but feeling sort of dishonest, "it's not like I've never been to school before. I do go lots of times. I go more than I don't go, in fact."

"Yes, but this is different, isn't it? You're motivated now, for whatever your brother has done." She reached over and smoothed Duane's hair. He looked a little guilty. "You *want* to go to school today, whereas lately if you went at all it was just barely, just temporary. What this is, this is *hope*. That's all I ask, really, is a little bit of hope."

The doorbell rang and I felt my face get a little flushed. I saw it in my brother's face too as we kicked out our chairs and started to go. How could we tell her now that I was hot not for school but for Duane's girlfriend?

"Who could that be?" Ma said.

"My ride," Duane said. "You know, Ma, maybe hope isn't all it's cracked up to be. You know, I mean, if you're happy right now, that could be good enough. I figure the purpose of today is to enjoy today." We were both backing out the door as he said it.

Ma was shaking her head. "You'll find out when you get older. The purpose of today is to get to tomorrow, and that's about it."

Dad passed us as we left, but the three of us barely noticed each other. I was so instantly sad after Ma said that, even the thought of Martha on the other side of the door couldn't pull me up.

"You know the barber asked me yesterday if I wanted him to trim my eyebrows," Dad said in a hurt, confused voice before we closed the door.

"Is it my birthday?" Martha joked. "Ain't I the doubly blessed."

Duane kissed her, and I managed to stammer, "Good morning." There was practically no talk during the twenty-minute ride in Martha's old Jeep CJ-7. Duane was staring off. Brooding, he'd call it.

"From that one I expect it," she said, pointing her thumb over her shoulder at me in the back. "But you, Duane sweetie, you give me the chills when you're not flappin' your gums."

"Sorry, Martha, I'll get better," he said, but didn't say anything more. She turned up the radio and let it do the talking for the rest of the ride. I stared into the rearview mirror at her exquisite, high-arching, caramel-colored, smooth-as-glass forehead.

"Thanks a lot, sweetheart," Duane said as he got out. "I'll call you this afternoon." I stayed in the back. Duane poked his head back inside. "You coming?" he said.

"No, I'm not," I said, just discovering my feelings

as they came out of my mouth.

Little Martha had swung around to face me. Now she turned back to Duane. "What do you think?"

"I am not my brother's keeper," he said, as he had said many times before. He always said that was the motto on our family's coat of arms. Only this time he said it with nothing funny in it.

"Well don't expect no chauffeuring," she said to me. "Get in the front seat."

"So, where you going?" we both said at the same time.

"I have to get to work," she said. "Over at the hospital. You going anywhere near there?"

"I am," I said, then thought about where I would go. She tooled along in the Jeep, taking corners too fast—I'm sure two wheels left the ground at least once. She giggled at that. She would take the occasional glance at me and smile, or shake her head in wonder. When she noticed her driving was making me grip the sides of my seat, she laughed a little more, at my stress. Just like Duane. But she reached over and gently patted my knee to calm me. To my surprise, it did just that.

"You really ain't much of a one for the chitchat, are you?" she said. "So, what do you do with yourself, Mr. Not Goin' to School Not Stayin' Home Not Talkin' 'Bout It Man? It doesn't seem to me you'd be the type to be hangin' on the corner or boostin' cars or nothin', like most of your truant criminal peers would be up to."

"I'm not a criminal, and those people are not my peers," I said coldly.

"I see," she said, smiling a big brilliant smile at herself in the rearview as she checked her fuchsia lipstick. "You're different. You're the quiet, sensitive James Dean–type truant criminal that nobody understands."

We were just approaching the cemetery, my cemetery, when Little Martha said all this. For a second she had me thinking, for the first time, was I like all the other aimless bums roaming the streets during the day? The heat was returning in my ears, like at those moments I can't control. I could hear my pulse thumping on my eardrums. But when my cemetery rolled into view, the gentle white-on-green of the stone-speckled hills like a cool cloth to my burning head, I knew it wasn't like that. I was not the same as *them*.

"I'll show you something," I said. "You want to see what I do?"

Martha looked at her watch. "I've got a few," she said. "Show me what you got."

I directed her to the parking lot at Gormely's.

When we walked down through the bulkhead,

Martha said, "What, do you have dead-mingling privileges? I guess this explains why you're so white, anyway." She laughed, but she kept looking all around her, as if she was expecting bats or something.

McLaughlin was stooped over behind a closed casket, sweeping a dead rat into the dustpan. His stick, with a bloodied tip, leaned on the wall next to him. When he straightened and turned to us with the rat like it was on his dinner plate, Martha gasped and walked a few steps back. McLaughlin looked just as surprised to see her.

"Well, well, hello, sister," he said. He went from being totally thrown to being the gracious host in a blink, with a facial change probably nobody but me would have noticed.

"Who's your lady friend there, boy?" As he spoke, he walked to the trash barrel, let the rodent slide in, then dusted off his hands. Like he was emerging from the shadows—which I suppose he was—he came over, bowed, and kissed Martha's hand. I had no idea till then he was suave.

"She's my *brother's* lady friend," I said with more open disappointment than I intended. Little Martha smiled at me like she already knew, and it was okay.

"You just compliment that brother of yours for me, first thing," he said, looking at Martha while he said it. McLaughlin's way, and the fact that things don't seem to bother Martha for too long, caused her to loosen right up.

"I understand you *live* here?" she said. She looked all around the softly glowing cellar, at the two caskets stacked against the far wall and the one on a sort of gurney in the middle of the room.

"This is home," he said, adding, "My, you are a beautiful lady."

"Thank you, but what do you do here? I mean, are you a mortician?"

Neither one of them was paying much attention to me, so I walked off to look.

"I care for the people who's brought here," McLaughlin said with pride. "I dress 'em. I pose 'em. I *present* 'em. I give them their dignity. You know, sister, like when you want to look real good for the world because you got a party to go to or a nice job or just because you got a *need*, to give y'self some respect." He tapped himself loudly on the chest with a long, stony index finger. "Well *I* do that for *them*." He pointed to the casket.

"Hey, Martha, so what do you think?" I called from my reclined position inside the top one of the caskets against the wall. I had removed my shoes, that's the rule, and was nestling down in the soft satin.

She gave me a very forced smile, and McLaughlin threw me a cold, mean, frighteningly dark stare, like

I'd never seen before. I felt stupid and small, perverse, as I climbed down. Even though I'd been in there fifty times before without feeling anything like that.

"I gotta get to work, Eric," Martha said as she shook McLaughlin's hand. "It was nice meeting you, Mr. McLaughlin. You do fine, important work here."

He smiled at her broadly, stiffly, before bowing and kissing her hand once more.

Little Martha walked up the bulkhead steps. I told McLaughlin I'd see him later and hurried to catch up to her. When I was about four steps up, I felt the grip on my arm, and he yanked me all the way back down. I shook a little as I looked into the menace of McLaughlin's face. His grasp was bruising my arm, I could feel, as his clawlike hand wrapped around my whole biceps, strong like no other sixty-one-year-old on earth.

"Don't you never, *never*, bring no goddamn woman down here again," he said in a bottomless deep voice.

He let go and silently motioned for me to leave.

"That was a lot of laughs, Eric." Little Martha chuckled as she raced the Jeep's engine. "Can I take you someplace?"

I didn't look up from the pavement of the parking lot as I walked right past her. "I'll walk," I said.

COMFORT 'EM UP

I BROKE A NEW CHRISTIAN BROTHERS hockey stick. I broke it on somebody's head. He was a teammate of mine. A friend, sort of, someone I pass to occasionally. It was only practice. There was some blood, but I think he was all right. The funny part is I don't really remember being that angry.

After he got up, the kid screamed all over the place about me being some kind of animal and how somebody better do something about me.

Coach said it was an accident. That I was carrying my stick too high, was all. I shouldn't do that anymore. It was just practice. It was an accident, and that's that. But none of my teammates will talk to me.

It was an accident because I'm an excellent hockey player, a lot better than the guy whose bell I rang. I feel bad about it, but I bet another guy would feel a lot worse. It's like I *know*, in my head, that I feel bad, but I don't quite *feel*, in my guts, that I feel bad.

The kid screamed at me, when he got his marbles back, that I was too violent for hockey. Too violent? For hockey? What's left if you're too violent for hockey? The zoo? The electric chair?

"You're just so intelligent, Eric," my mother said. "I can't understand why you behave so strangely. I have no idea what motivates you."

My mother's reason for concluding that I'm some kind of brain is that I don't talk much and I don't have friends. People assume that if you don't talk, you're either a genius or a simpleton. Being my mother, she really doesn't have any choice but to think it's the first thing, not the second. The fact is I have a nothing but ordinary level of intelligence. So ordinary that sometimes it makes me want to scream, or burst into flames from the inside. I wish instead that I was so damn smart that it just didn't matter to me, or so stupid that I didn't know.

"Don't overreact, Marion," my father said as he sat down to breakfast. He sat across the small circular table from me and smiled awkwardly. Not a curled smile, but a flat, slanted one like the wings of an airplane making a turn. "I'm sure Eric didn't hit that boy on purpose. Right, son?" He didn't wait for a response, which was good because there wasn't one coming. "They're on the same team, for god's sake."

Ma continued to work the stove, the sink, the re-frigerator, always with her back to the humans in the room. "Don't make excuses for him."

"I'm not," Dad said. He gave me a wink. I couldn't tell if he was happy because he got to play good cop to Ma's bad, or because of the little thrill he got every time I clocked somebody. I've seen that, when I play hockey, football, lacrosse, anything with contact. More than any other phase of the game, Dad would always go ape when I nailed somebody. It got worse and worse every year, and I started to think that it wasn't all part of the game, like he said it was. I think sometimes he'd like to use me for a day, to take me around with my stick and point people out, say-ing, "There, conk my boss. Crack that guy who cut me off. Spear that dog. Brain your mother."

"Richard," Ma snapped. "Say something to him."

Dad was buttering some toast. I was eating my raisin bran. "All right." He sort of waved her off. Without her seeing it, of course. "Eric, carry your stick a little lower, will you?"

I just smiled and nodded. Then I could tell from the way he looked over my shoulder that Duane was coming up behind me. Dad stood to take his toast and coffee to the car with him. Ma hadn't seen Duane yet.

"And . . . ?" she prodded Dad.

"And . . ." He thought. "Oh yes. And stay out of the cemetery, huh?" This was apparently a talk they had discussed in advance. As much as they discuss anything, that is.

"Fine, Dad, no cemetery," I said.

"Hello, Duane," Dad said as he left. It occurred to me that my parents should never say "Hello, Duane"; they should always say "Good-bye, Duane" when they see him.

Duane patted me on the shoulder on the way by and I flinched. When I looked up, he was sitting in the seat next to me, with my hockey helmet on. I laughed and went to punch him on the shoulder but he cowered, covering up his face and shrinking into the chair. "No, no," he pleaded. I then reached to pick up my spoon again, and he covered up. I reached for the sugar bowl, and he covered up.

Ma turned around and looked at him. "Hello, Duane," she said, and left.

I did not go to the cemetery.

"Did you ever hit anybody, McLaughlin?" I said as he tucked a body into the coffin. "I mean, really pound somebody, like if they didn't get up again you wouldn't have minded. Ever do that?"

McLaughlin stopped his tucking, leaning on the

body as he thought about it. The dead guy wouldn't have minded, though, a big, robust, barrel-chested guy who looked like he had no business being dead. I don't think McLaughlin had to think too hard about what his answer was; it was more whether he wanted to give it.

"Knocked out a few in my day," he said, without pride, or regret, or anything else. "Prob'ly more than I should have, but not as many as I wanted to." He looked off for a few seconds, then went back to work.

"Ya, well, I've knocked out a few too. But for me it's both—not as many as I've wanted to, and a lot more than I've wanted to. I mean, I don't want to hit anybody, most of the time, but then there are moments when I want to take my hockey stick like a sickle and just mow down everybody in my path."

I stopped, waiting for a reaction from McLaughlin. He gave me exactly the same response as the guy in the box. Which is why, I suppose, I could talk to McLaughlin in the first place.

"I don't always have very strong reasons for flipping out. It's just . . . that I get tense, and I can't think of anything else to do. I'm not crazy, you know, McLaughlin, but the few people who do talk to me speak to me like I'm the guy in the supermarket with a gun and fifty hostages."

There was a tiny crack of a smile on McLaughlin's

face. "Cain't get along," he said. "It ain't unusual, that a person cain't get along with his other fellow persons. It's your method, though, that's got people worried. But it don't got to be that way. Look at me. I couldn't get along neither, that's why I'm here." He looked down into the dead man's face and gently stroked the forehead, like he was helping him to sleep.

"I simply never got the knack for dealing with people who could talk back to me. And I got into trouble all the time, 'cause I couldn't deal. That's why I eventually come here. This I can deal with, better than most. I take care of these people. I can do for them what they need, and I can keep everything under control too, down in this world here."

McLaughlin motioned me to come closer. When I did, he slammed the top of the coffin closed. "That's right, a *coffin*," he said. "This ain't no casket. This man and his kin understand. A person don't need to go under in one of them big silky Cadillac boxes to hide in. *This*"—he walked all the way around the box, sliding his hand over it, caressing it—"it's got narrow feet down the bottom, and big wide shoulders up here just like the cowboy inside. Then it tapers off again at the head. It's *people* shaped, man. It says, 'There's a people in here, junior, and don't you ever forget it.' The folks who ordered this care a lot about how we take care of their man, and I'm here to see that he's taken care of, 'cause maybe I'm the only one who really will."

He threw the coffin open again, this time opening both halves of the lid. "Otherwise," he said, pulling up the sheet that revealed the man's bare feet, even though he was all dressed in his suit, "you get nothing but this." He pointed at the feet, and I looked up close. They looked as if someone had been working them with a chisel. Square chunks gone off the instep and heel, both big toes half gone and showing bone. But almost no blood, since it had been drained already.

"We got rats," McLaughlin said, like he was admitting something shameful about his home.

I stepped away. "So what do you do about it?"

"It's a little late now," he said, shaking his head. He stroked the man's forehead again, then let his hand rest there as he looked into the face. "Usually I don't sleep through the rat attacks. I do a lot of stick chasin'. But once in a while . . . a man gets tired, y'know. . . . You know what the dudes upstairs in the suits say? They say 'Don't worry about it, pal. Happens in every home in the city.' They say 'What's the big deal? *He* don't feel it, and it don't show once you get their shoes on or plaster on a little makeup.'"

From the side I could see McLaughlin's jaw

muscles flexing. "Comfort 'em up. That's what I do now, boy. Just comfort 'em up. These is *my* people down here."

At that moment he seemed so right. Down there in that cellar under the yellow light, McLaughlin and the dead people were a good fit. He needed them and they needed him, and it seemed that nobody else in the world wanted either of them.

I could do that, I thought. I could manage here, with these people. "McLaughlin, could I . . . ?"

"You gotta go now, boy," he said in a whisper, as he continued to look into the dead man's face.

VISION

"**I**F I KNOW ONE THING in this world, this is the thing I know," Duane said. "The reason you're a psychopath is that you're a prisoner." He had his nose pressed up against the glass of Mary's cage while he talked. He was watching me dangle a mouse in front of her mouth.

"Am I, Duane? Really, a psychopath?"

"Sure you are," he said, but he didn't say it with any meanness or judgment in it. "Look at you, Eric. You're like the Birdman of Alcatraz in here."

At that moment Mary snagged the mouse. She whipped it against the glass, right in front of Duane's nose, then bit so hard that she cut the mouse in half, the back end falling out of her mouth.

"Ho-lee shit," Duane whooped, clapping and laughing a nervous laugh. Then he scurried over to my fish tank. "What about these guys, Eric? Do they do anything outrageous like that?"

"No, stupid, they're fish. Leave 'em alone. Leave me alone too. I'm not a prisoner. I go wherever I want and do whatever I want."

"No you don't," he said. "You do mental things that you can't help. You hide in here. You run away. You play sports. And above all, you keep your mouth shut."

"So?" I said, elbowing him out of the way so I could feed my fish.

"So," he said in his very rare "serious" voice, "I think you got something to say."

I didn't say anything.

"Eric?" Duane said after I'd fed the fish for about a minute, probably asphyxiating them with flakes.

"Maybe I just like to be quiet," I said.

Duane went into a pitch-perfect imitation of our father. "'Suck it up, boy.' 'Take it like a man.' 'No bellyaching.' 'Oh, you'll be all right, that didn't hurt.' And don't forget his immortal bathroom advice, 'If you shake it more than once, you're playing with it.' You know how many times I shake it when I go in there now? . . ."

"I don't want to hear about it, Duane."

"Hey, there's another one—'I don't want to hear about it.'"

"No, Duane, that was me. I wasn't imitating Dad.

I meant *I* don't want to hear about it."

"See, Eric, I was right, you're just like they are."

"No I'm not. You don't know anything about me, so just shut up."

"Very good, 'Shut up' is another one. But wait. Now that I think about it, I think 'I don't want to hear about it' was Ma's saying, not Dad's. That's right, she was 'I don't want to hear about it.' Dad was 'I don't want to *talk* about it.' Or was it 'I don't give a flying fuck'? Oh no, that one was me."

Duane was having such a good time that he didn't even notice that I had flopped on my bed, my forearm drawn across my eyes. When he noticed, he came over. He placed a hand lightly on my chest. I jumped up.

"Don't do that, Duane, please," I said. "You know I don't like to be touched. I just don't like it, okay?"

"Okay," he whispered, like he was talking a jumper down. "I was just trying—"

"I know," I said. And I *did* know. I knew he was trying to help me loosen up. I knew that my brother really was my friend and that he was putting his hand on me to tell me that in his own way. But the difference between *knowing* it and *feeling* it . . . for me it was a leap across the falls.

"It's almost time," Ma hummed from the doorway. Church.

Duane was kneeling beside my bed, as if he was giving me last rites. "You don't really want to go, do you?" he whispered. I shook my head. "Then say it. Tell her, Eric. You'll feel better, I promise."

"What are you saying over there?" Ma said.

He didn't even turn toward her. "Just getting him prepped for church. I told him the truth shall set him free."

Ma growled something to Duane about not blaspheming, but I wasn't listening to her. He was at my ear again. "C'mon, Eric, I've been there, I know what you're feeling. Speak up to her. Don't you want to be like me?"

He was half joking with that last one. But only half. Duane seemed so strong to me, so together, so sure. Didn't I want to be like him? I had no idea what I wanted. But I knew I couldn't start being like Duane just because Duane said it was cool. I just couldn't.

I did know that I didn't want to go to church, though.

I went to church.

"Isn't this nice, eh?" my mother said to my father as he drove to church. His name is Richard but she calls him 'Eh' more often than not. Not Richie, Rick, or the dreaded "Dickie," but "Eh." "Eh? Don't you think it's wonderful, having the whole family together for something like this?" It was like she was challenging us to point out that there was one son missing, kind of blowing the "whole family" deal. But Duane didn't fit the picture, so Ma wasn't above airbrushing him out, like an old Soviet dictator. Besides, she *knew* neither Dad nor I would challenge her version.

"Ya," Dad said as he searched the radio dial for anything but Sunday-morning preaching. He looked stiffer about all this than me.

A big fat mouse galloped across my shoes as I sat in the pew. Quite unmouselike because he was so obese, he seemed to take forever clomping his way up over one shoe, down the other side, across the space between my feet, up the other shoe . . .

I snatched him up in my hand. And, I guess, I laughed out loud. I don't know what had my mother more mortified, the rodent or her son, but she shrank from both of us, elbowing my father fifty times before he finally snapped out of his weekend trance that he always wore except for hockey weekends. She pointed at the mouse furiously. Dad seemed like he had to fix his eyes on it for a few seconds before he could lock onto what was going on. But when he did, a strange, not-too-bad thing happened. He smiled a little. I realized then, though it had always been apparent I suppose, that he almost never smiled. Not for real anyway.

He smiled at me, and he smiled at my mouse, like

he was glad to see us. Then, after one more, more frantic dig in his ribs from Ma, he winced and gave me a gentle wave to say, "Go ahead, put it down."

So I did, but I didn't like it. That would have fed Mary for a week. Dad could have told her to lighten up, get off the kid's back. No, he couldn't have. I dashed the mouse hard to the marble floor. Where it stayed. Until I kicked it under a pew.

I tried to pay attention to the mass, but it was hopeless. Most of the words that filtered through my ears I'd heard a billion times before as a kid. "Blessed are the meek. . . . Blessed are the peacemakers. . . . I believe. . . . I believe. . . . Hallowed be thy name. . . . I believe. . . . Lamb of God, you take away the sins of the world. . . . I believe. . . . Have mercy on us. . . . I shall not want. . . ." But it was all like just so much nothing. I *did* want. I just didn't know *what* I wanted, except that I wanted a vision like Duane had. A million times he told me about the "vision" he had on the football field that forever changed him from a brainless, sports-playing feeb like me into the guitar-playing, cool wise guy he is today. He was my age when he had his vision, and I still hadn't had mine, so I was even willing to take a whack at the prayer thing to get it, but I wasn't hopeful.

Every few seconds Ma would lean into me and nudge, gesturing at the priest and nodding, to say,

"How 'bout *that* one. Did you catch *that* beaut?" I just smiled, weaved in and out of light sleep, occasionally pulling the dead mouse back out with my foot so I could look at him. When something's dead, I can't help looking at it.

I didn't hear, actually hear, any of the service until the second reading. That I heard because the priest *screamed* the first word. "ASK! and it shall be given you; seek, and ye shall find; knock, and it shall be opened unto you."

My mother didn't call this one to my attention. It grabbed me all on its own. I absently rolled the mouse's carcass back under the bench and stared at the priest. Is that it? I thought. Is this maybe *my* vision? Is that all I have to do to knock out the crazies, to stop being a prisoner like Duane said I was? Just open my mouth? Seek? Ask? Knock? Is that possible? Does anybody actually want to listen? I turned to my mother, but she didn't notice me. I leaned to look at my father, but his brain was on ice. On the ice in St. Louis in April of 1970, when Bobby Orr scored the overtime goal to win the Bruins the Stanley Cup. I looked back at the priest. *He* sure looked sure, as he prepared for Communion.

Communion. That would be it. That would be the test. If I was going to have a vision—God, please let me have some kind of vision, anything, so I can be hard and in control like Duane, not mental and tense—it would certainly be over Communion. Church is where normal people have visions all the time. Maybe there was a normal person trying to gnaw his way out through my chest, and that's why I get the pounding in there like I get.

I queued up like everybody else, inched my way along, hands folded. I smiled at all the people walking back after receiving, without chewing, their bread. *Everybody* stared and gave me a curious, nervous smile. Was I not supposed to be here? Was I frightening people? Oh no, *that* was my "community" Ma brought me here for. Of course: community, Communion. Com-munity, Com-munion. This was it, it *had* to be it, my vision. Please let this be my vision.

It was my turn and I took it. On the tongue, the old-fashioned way, rather than in my hand. If there was anything extra to be tasted off the priest's finger, I was getting it first-hand, not wasted on my palm. He mumbled, I nodded, he placed the wafer gently on my tongue.

I felt a rush as I walked back along the red rug of the center aisle. It had been a long time since I'd done this, and the first time I'd done it as part of a Revelation. I felt like everyone was watching me change from Saul to Paul, although they might just have been staring because my being there was like when somebody's Doberman follows them into the church, cute but frightening. I didn't care, though, because I was alone at that moment with . . .

My vision? I rolled the wafer around on my tongue, trying to feel it. To feel what, carbonation? Heat? Broken glass? I hadn't a clue, but goddamn it I wasn't going to let it slip away. It must have been ten minutes I kept that wafer trapped in my mouth, because I *wanted* it. It stuck like tape to my tongue. Then it turned to mush. But I wouldn't give it up. I was afraid whatever it was I was seeking, I might miss it.

Finally, long after I sat back on the pew, I had to swallow. What I felt going down was Styrofoam. And when it landed in my belly, instead of the fire of the Holy Spirit, I felt the growling hollowness that was there before.

I looked around at my new community and nobody was looking at me anymore. I don't really know that they ever were. I slid down in the pew and looked at my father, who hadn't gone to Communion. He looked at his watch. My mother was kneeling down, eyes welded shut, her lips moving frantically to pray, like stupid people do when they read. Maybe I didn't know what a vision was exactly, but I knew this wasn't it. I kneeled down next to my mother, which gave her a little smile. But instead of praying, I slid my hand slickly along the floor, found the plump, soft, warm-but-cooling body, and dropped it in my coat pocket. Vision, I don't know crap about. But this little creature's life running out into my pocket—that I could feel.

When nobody said anything on the way home— Ma merely smiled that personal, religious smile, Dad burrowed into the steering wheel and the radio—I tried one more feeble shot at jump starting my vision.

"He didn't *scream* it." Ma sounded annoyed. "He said it just as audibly and distinctly as all the other fine words."

"Well anyway," I said, "to me, it sounded like he was encouraging people to speak up. To communicate with each other. You know, 'to ask, to knock,' to . . . talk."

She spoke to me from the front seat without turning around. Her tone was somewhere between someone whose favorite movie had been interrupted by a dumb question and someone who had to give directions to a person who didn't speak the same language.

"Seek, Eric. And *ye* shall find. I think it means that you need to figure things out for yourself. 'God takes care of those who take care of themselves' is what he was telling you."

I thought about it for a second. Dad turned up the radio on a Drifters song, "Under the Boardwalk."

"But don't you think," I said, "that we'd be better

off airing it out, discussing——"

"Religion is a private affair," Ma snapped. "Each person must work out his feelings for himself, with God."

There was no mistaking that this conversation was over. She acted like I wanted to talk about her underwear, or the sex lives of her nun friends at the convent. I fingered the mouse in my pocket and shut up. More than ever, I realized, I did want to be like Duane. When we got home, I was going to tell him so.

As we silently wafted over the living-room threshold, we were stopped by Duane's voice, which seemed to have an unusual lilt. He was draped sideways over the big armchair reading—the Bible? He'd picked up the one Ma forced on me.

"This ain't a half-bad book, you know," he said. "Jeremiah sucks, but Ecclesiastes and Revelation, while a little confused, are some pretty hot shit."

Ma *ran* to snatch the book away from Duane. "Cast not pearls before swine," she said. Dad walked right by them and snapped on the TV. I stood staring at Duane, who had obviously actually *read* some of the book while we were gone.

Just when I thought I had *somebody* figured out. I didn't know anything.

L'ANIMAL

MONTREAL. APRIL. Must be fifty feet of snow. "Hockey Night in Canada" is on every TV in the city. *The* tournament in all of North America. Dad couldn't stop smiling. Pulled me out of school on Wednesday, two days early and one of which I was planning to attend, to get up here and get acclimated. It worked, I guess, because we won our opener the first morning, mostly because of me. I was pretty savage, and that's by my own admission. I was hurting, and I wanted to take a nap. Dad wanted to take me to the hotel restaurant—the same hotel where practically every team was staying—and buy me a big steak.

I don't know if he wore his Bruins jacket to piss everybody off on purpose, but it was working. It's as if every last person in Quebec hated our guts, and my father was loving every minute of it.

"They can't *stand* that we don't speak French," he

chuckled across the table. I was hardly listening to him. I was looking at the looks. I was getting looks all over the place. It's a different thing up here. Hockey's not taken lightly, the way it is back home. Here, a little peewee nobody dink like me, even hidden deep inside a face mask and oversized pads, can be picked out of a crowd eating his steak. And they remember every cheap shot you threw, every hip check, every blind pass that made their baby Gretzkys corkscrew themselves into the ice. But Dad was certain it was really his English and his Bruins insignia with the big spoked B that got everybody hot. He wore his jacket all through the meal.

"In seventy and seventy-two," he said, grinning like he had something to do with it, "the 'Big Bad Bruins' were *it*, the scourge of the NHL. Orr, Esposito, Hodge, Cashman, Cheevers, MacKenzie, Sanderson, Don Awrey . . . we were incredible, you should have seen it, Eric."

We. *We* were incredible, he said. I didn't know what to say.

"That was a long time ago, huh Dad?"

"It wasn't that long ago," he snapped, even though I wasn't even *born* by 1972. "The *Rangers* haven't won the cup since 1940—now that's a long time. And another thing, the Bruins could have won it a lot of times since if it wasn't for flukes, dumb coaching, and idiot linesmen." Dad was gesturing at me with his knife, with a big chunk of basically raw meat dripping off the end. Whenever we're away, he insists they leave his meat raw. He started mumbling as he put the food in his mouth, and I'm not sure what event he was referring to, though I'd heard it many times. "Too many men on the ice," he growls. "Too many men on the goddamn ice. Cherry. Don Fathead Cherry . . ."

It always happens this way. It's the raw beef, I think, that makes him crazy.

"Goon," I heard from somewhere in the restaurant as we headed out. I looked around to see who said it, and everyone in the place looked like they said it. It seemed like every table and booth was full of players from the tournament with their families, including some of my teammates. Nobody, nobody looked friendly, and they were all looking back at us. My dad laughed and waved at them all. I turned away.

"Say good-bye to *l'Animal*," we heard amid laughs and boos as we left.

"They respect you. They fear you, son," Dad said as he squeezed my shoulders as hard as he could. "I'm very proud. You should be proud."

I was not proud. I would want to boo *l'Animal* myself. But they tell me the animal *is* myself.

We walked through the tournament on the way to the final game. I was potting goals like it was just my street-hockey net in the driveway with nobody there to stop me. Nobody would admit it, I'm sure, but I think guys were giving me the wide berth all week-end because of my reputation. That makes me madder than anything. Usually in these north-of-the-border games, I run into at least one nutty ranch beast from Nowhere, Alberta, who doesn't care diddly about who I am or who I think I am or who the crowd or my father thinks I am, who has nothing else on his tiny little farm-boy mind except to separate me from the puck, my jock, and my senses every chance he gets. It is on those occasions that my team doesn't get out of the first or second round, and when I leave the city I leave behind some little gift, a reminder that I have passed through on my way to obscurity, like maybe a pint of blood, or some of my hair still caught under farm boy's fingernails.

Those are the times when my team is pissed off at me because we lost, and my father talks fight during the whole trip back over whatever tundra we've crossed, and I'm sore enough to lie on the shower-room floor and stay there for the winter. But I think, as I drift off in the front seat of the car. I think of the farm boy, his determination, his knuckles bouncing off my lumpy forehead, his apparent certainty that he has a job to do in this life and he's gonna goddamn well do it. And I smile. Even as I sleep, I know I'm smiling.

Guys like that, though, you don't usually find them on the Quebec teams. Those teams are somehow always filled with twenty-five guys who can skate faster, shoot harder, and make plays prettier than every single American kid you've ever faced off against. They don't have much interest in the rough stuff. They have no need.

Which is why, in the tournament finals against Montreal's finest, we were down 9–1 in the third period with five minutes left. The one goal we had wasn't mine, but in a way it was. Our defenseman was lining up for a shot out at the blue line, and I was doing the dirty work in front of the net. The score was already 6–0, and it was pretty clear that just about my whole team had packed it in, so the defensemen spent all their time bottling me up, because I hadn't figured out yet that we couldn't win.

It was your basic pinball game in front of the goalie, with these two big defensemen taking turns bouncing me back and forth from one corner of the crease to the other. Our point men passed the puck back and forth looking for the best shot. My wingers, stouthearted bastards that they are, were sort of floating along the boards reading the French advertisements for tires and spring water. After one-two-three-four bing-bings off these guys' big shoulders and the referees' generous hometown non-involvement, I got dizzy, disoriented. Trying to keep my balance—and nothing more, I swear—I jabbed my stick out, a thrust, really.

I speared the goalie, in the cup. He dropped to the ice like a puffy snowman melting inside the bulky goalie's equipment. My defenseman looked a little stunned to see all that open net but finally slapped the puck in, though not like he enjoyed it or anything.

It was a nasty crowd. But I think they hated the officials more than me at that point. Because the referee and two linesmen were so busy letting the locals give me the rattling I deserved, they were in no position to see my accident. They couldn't do anything about it, and the crowd was loud and merciless about it.

As I approached the bench, my team was subdued. The coach didn't say anything. I heard some names—animal, pig, stiff, goon, psycho, and a lot of French words that sounded horrible no matter how they translated—from the stands. I looked up at my dad three rows behind our bench. He was ecstatic, howling, both fists raised. From the row behind, someone dumped a giant Coke right over his head, and he didn't flinch. He just spread his arms wider and turned his open palms up, like welcoming a refreshing spring rain.

"I'm gonna keel you." I was startled by the voice, mostly because it was the only one that had actually spoken to me face to face—other than my dad, which hardly counted—the whole four days I was in Montreal.

"Huh?" I said, still a little rattled.

"When your ass comes back on the ice, you're a dead man," he said again with the thick, halting French accent. I nodded, like I always do when people tell me that. I thought nothing of it because the guy saying it, a guy named Rejan Houle, was a star, not a fighter. Even among stars he was a star. Out of the nine goals his team had, he had six. He never fought *anybody*, never mind having a go with *me*.

Coach heard the threat, and before I could even get a squeeze off the Gatorade bottle, I was back, wobbly-legged, on the ice. He was actually giving me up to the bloodthirsty horde.

But like I say, I thought absolutely nothing of it. When you hear that stuff as much as I do, it flies by. Which is why, when it came, I was floored. Literally.

The ref threw the puck down, and as I watched it hit the ice, I watched the gloved hand come rocketing up. *Wham!* Houle threw a textbook uppercut that sent my head snapping back so hard that you could hear the echo all over the rink when my helmet met the ice. And he was on me. Holding my shirt with his right, he pummeled me with five, six crisp left hands before I could roll him over.

As we grappled to our feet, I had already left my gift to Montreal. Spit. Two upper-right-side teeth skittering like tiny bloody figure skaters across the ice.

But I had to trade. Bang, bang, bang, bang, bang, I could feel him get heavier in my grip with every shot I landed on his fleshy, purple nose. As his knees bent and he began to slide to the ice, I thought he was out, hoped he was out. I just wanted to go home. Houle's teammates stood around us in a semicircle in case I got out of line. My teammates stood about thirty feet away, lined up in front of the bench talking about where to eat on the way home. The officials stood a couple of feet off, "Letting 'em go," as they say when they don't want to admit that they like the blood as much as anybody.

I was delivering Houle to the ice, no longer punching—stupid, breaking my own safety rule—just lowering him by his shirt since he seemed almost unconscious. Suddenly he shocked me. Seizing my head with both hands, he pulled me down, my face right to his, and bit. I watched up close, like on some freaky cable medical program, as his mouth opened, then clamped down on the bridge of my nose. First the sight of his gaping throat, then of my own spraying blood exploding in the small space between us, had me paralyzed. I dropped to the ground and lay on my side.

I never heard such an ovation. Houle got to his feet and skated toward the dressing room to the sound of thunder. Foot stomping and howling filled my head as the ref came to check me. I waved him off, pushed him, actually, even though I was bleeding like a faucet and I really could have used his help.

The game was over for me, of course. As the assistant coach walked me off to go get stitched, I paused. I looked up into the stands and listened to two thousand people screaming at me, laughing, some of them, pounding their fists gleefully on the Plexiglas as I passed. For the first time ever it sank in: People, grown-up people and kids alike, were cheering because I was hurt. Hurt bad, like in a car accident. I felt tinier than one of my teeth, which were still out there somewhere skipping around on the vast white ice. I looked up for my dad, kind of like Jim Craig did in the 1980 Olympics. But he was gone.

Blood from somewhere on my forehead was running into my eyes, blinding me, as I was led off.

_____

The assistant coach, who is also trainer and medical man, sprayed me with something to numb me up before the stitching. So all I felt as he worked the thread in and out between my eyes was a small tugging. While he worked, I stared into space, playing my tongue in and out of the new, slimy spaces on the right side of my mouth.

The locker room was big and chilling, in the basement of the old auditorium. The white-tiled floor and walls, under harsh fluorescent lights, maybe made it seem larger and colder than it was. But the real thing of it, probably, was the nobodyness of it. Just me and the trainer, stitching me silently, like he was just putting somebody's name on the back of a sweater while I stared into his pointy chin. I don't know why that should bother me. It just seems like when there's a lot of your own blood on your shirt, the floor, crusting in the corners of your mouth, that there should also be a lot of people around you who maybe give a damn.

I don't know—it doesn't matter. At least I felt no pain. I didn't feel anything at all, honestly.

"Hey."

Until then. The voice cut through the quiet like the crack a slapshot makes in an empty rink. It was Rejan Houle.

"How are you?" he said, approaching as if he had just stumbled across me, a wreck in the street, and he wanted to help.

"Are you for real?" I said, pulling away from the trainer.

"Jesus, you guys aren't going to pull out all my stitchwork now, are you?" the trainer said with the greatest concern.

Houle put out both hands like a traffic cop. "No, no, no, no. That's over with." He turned to me. "Is it not, my friend?"

I had to laugh out loud. "Your friend? Give me a break. *My* friends don't bite me in the face," I lied. My best friend was Mary the water dragon, who, as a matter of fact, bit my face more than once.

"Listen, I'm sorry about that. But that was my brother you speared." The way he said the word— "brodder"—sounded special. "I can't let nobody hurt Benny. I love my brother."

"So let me get this straight," the trainer said. "You guys ain't going to be taking any more dings out of each other? You're here to make kissy face this time? Because if not . . ." He gestured upstairs to where the game was still going on.

"If you like," said Houle, "I could take a hunk out of *your* nose. I'm still kind of hungry."

"Ya, go ahead, get out of here," I said. "Don't stay on my account."

As the trainer left, Houle stuck his hand out and gripped mine, the same hands we'd hurt on each other's faces. We shook gently. "You're not a bad hockey player," he said. "For an American hacker."

I hopped off the table, where I was sitting in my underwear. I started pulling on my dungarees. "How would you know? I didn't play any hockey today. *You* did, though."

"No, I could see it. Your whole team quit, if I may say so. But you just kept going like"—he covered his mouth, holding in a snicker as long as he could—"like you thought you could *win*." And then he burst out laughing. I couldn't help myself. Like a yo-yo I joined him.

"God, did my team suck, or what?" I howled.

"You did, you did." Houle was doubled over. "And you know what else?"

I pulled my thick black Champion sweatshirt over my head, popped my head out like a turtle. "What?"

"You hate playing, don't you?"

"I do, I hate it, I hate it, I hate it . . ." I babbled. The laughter rolled along under its own power, that idiot laughter that needs nothing funny to fuel it but feels better than anything else in the world.

Giddy, I laced my sneakers but didn't tie them. Eventually the humor ran out and I had to talk. "You could tell, huh? That I don't like playing?"

"Hey, look at me." Houle made the sweeping

gesture that magicians make when doing a disappearing trick, passing a hand downward over his face, then running it past the front of his body. "Hockey is my life. I am hockey, and hockey is me. I love it, breathe it, know it better than anybody in Canada or anywhere else. You saw me play. Do you doubt that my life is going to be in hockey?"

I shook my head. I didn't doubt it for a second. Rejan Houle had the grit and sense of mission like the Alberta farm boys, only with a mountain of talent behind it.

"And it's because I love it the way I do that I can tell when somebody else doesn't love it. And brodder, you don't love it. I watched the games you *won* earlier in the tournament, and you got no pleasure from it." I stared at him as he said it, the nose I'd mangled for him bobbing up and down like a plum over his mouth. He knew hockey players like I knew lizards. I was glad—and shocked—that he came over to tell me.

"Thanks," I said as I slung my bag over my shoulder, carrying my sticks like rifles. My team had begun to slither into the locker room, but they were like ghosts to me. I hadn't the slightest interest in seeing them, and had no trouble looking through them.

"But you thought I was good, huh?" I said to Houle.

"Good?" he laughed, pretending to pick his teeth.

"Good? You were delicious."

I waved him off.

"Tell you the truth," he said while I walked away, "I can only imagine how good you would be if you *cared*. But for myself, I'm glad you don't." He laughed again. What was it that made him think everything was so riotous, just like Duane? "I'll talk to you again, friend."

There was that word again. It made me smile, but with my back to the room so nobody could see. "Sure," I said.

As I knew he would be, Dad was waiting outside the locker room. "How's the nose?" he said, dead as a telephone operator. As much as I know he loved the rough stuff, it did always seem to freak him when I was hurt. Like maybe *he* did it. His hair was all matted down by the Coke. When I said, "I'm fine," he took my bag.

We were almost out of Quebec on the long road home, which got longer with every trip we made, when my father spoke his first words.

"The trip was not a success, Eric," he groaned, ignoring the fact that my team came closer to winning the tournament than any New England team ever had.

I had been sleeping, and I didn't much care to talk about it anyway. My eyes hurt, I was beginning to miss my teeth, and the hard work I'd done during the earlier games was starting to come up as aches in the deepest regions of my muscles. "Um-hmm," I said, as if I was really being invited to join in anyway.

"This tournament ended on a decidedly down beat. But don't get discouraged. Your game will improve—you're too strong, you work too hard for it not to. And you need a better supporting cast. But by the time we come back up here next year . . ."

With every word he said, hockey—the sport, the game, the idea—slipped further out of my mind. He could have been talking about t'ai chi or shipbuilding at that moment, for all I could feel the points he was making. I could not even entertain the thought of making this trek one more year. Just like that, something I had done just about every day of my life in one form or another—tabletop hockey for hours at a time with anyone who'd play; ice hockey at three, five, six thirty A.M. or whenever we could get the rink time; street hockey in the driveway until the hard orange ball turned invisible in the darkness— was losing all meaning. I understood how Duane felt when he ran over every other freshman on the football field, then walked away for good.

I closed my eyes for the rest of the trip, and in my mind I walked away for good.

THIRD PERIOD

FAMOUS MEN

PUBLIC RELATIONS. My father's game. P.R. He's a publicist, he says. He got roasted one time at the annual dinner of the local advertising association. It might have been a big deal, except that about fifty other publicists were roasted at the same time, most of them fifteen years younger than my dad. It was one of the only times my mother and father went out of the house together. He wore a rented black tux, she wore a not altogether shabby copper-colored gown that she had to borrow from her sister. I swear they were smiling when they left. Dad's "roasting" amounted to one quick line about his cheesy rented suit, jammed in the middle of a slick, stupid, three-minute routine by a rented comic who had never laid eyes on him. They were home in under an hour, Ma pressing Dad with one of her headaches that kill everybody. "Either *I* have a headache, Richard, or *you* have one, but we're leaving before they serve the Cheese Whiz." No, I wasn't there. I know because Ma told me and Duane—and anybody else she saw that month—all about it very loudly. Like *he* had done something to *her*. All in good fun, he kept muttering into his cummerbund. Good for business. All through a smile that just didn't make it.

The perk of perks in his job, as far as Dad was concerned, was being able to rub up against people who are somewhat well known. Or who maybe were once well known. Or who may, possibly, perhaps with my father's help, someday be somewhat well known. "The Almost-Has-Beens and Near-Nobodies" is what Duane called them. More than making money, more than getting promoted, more than ever becoming a somebody of his own, Dad's purpose in his job seemed to be to get these people to come to our house for dinner.

And we all had to be there for these dinners. Except Duane, who had a standing invitation to *not* be there but rarely missed one of them. My mother, for all her complaining, seemed to anticipate these things more than anyone. Dad always kept it a surprise who he was bringing home, like we were all going to just die when we saw who it was. I think that, despite all the evidence, Ma kept waiting for Michael Jordan or Lee Iacocca to come for pot roast.

Instead we got people Dad described as little captains of industry. Like the Vermont guy who made the all-natural toothpaste and sold it for four dollars a tube all over the East. Turned out he needed a little P.R. assistance when people realized his paste was fifty percent maple syrup.

"I ask you," Dad said dramatically, waving a knife in one hand and a fork in the other. "Is there another substance on god's green earth that's as natural as maple syrup? Jeez." The "jeez" came with a big wide head shake that Dad always used to point out how crazy and unreasonable the world is.

"Ya, but you don't want to brush your *teeth* with it, for chrissake," Duane blurted.

Dad stared at Ma, who relayed the glare to Duane, who pretended not to see it.

Ma got busy removing all evidence of the meal. In a few minutes she returned, her wind back, with a ring cake and an enormous knife. "So, you did it all yourself?" she chirped as if all was hunky-dory. "No silver spoon in your mouth, am I right, Jerry?" In a sort of "Now for the musical portion of our show" deal, Dad always winds up yielding to Ma for our guests' rags-to-riches story or overcoming-handicaps story or plain-old-determination story. No slouch at the old spin control herself, Ma could take a Kennedy—if Dad could ever wrestle one home—and make him look like an overachiever. All in her search for inspirational role models. For me.

"*I'll* tell you about a real hero," Duane jumped in. He cut Jerry off right in the middle of humbly— they're *all* humble—telling his up-from-nowhere story. "I saw this guy in a club the other night, a drummer. Forget the fact that this guy was one of the most explosive backbeaters I've ever heard. The big deal is that the guy had no arms! I'm not lying. They had his whole kit spread on the ground in front of him and he worked them all with pedals, like they usually do with bass drums. You should have seen it—his feet were flying like a tap dancer on hot coals.

"It was inspirational, is what it was. The crowd was berserk for this guy. I tell you, if I knew how to cry, that's where I would have done it, right there."

There was a pause at the table all around.

"You went to a *club*?" Dad finally said.

"How old are you?" Jerry said.

Ma just shook her head and pressed her lips together until they disappeared. Then she asked Jerry more about his college days.

Like I said, Duane exaggerates. But he doesn't lie. So even if it was a one-armed drummer, that was a story and a half. I sat trying to picture the drummer, who would have been a whole lot more interesting a role model than the toothpaste guy.

"Anyone for dessert?" Dad slapped his hands together loudly and rubbed like he was all excited, even though he only ate dessert when we had company. And only if *they* ate it.

"I could go for a nice big bowl of toothpaste," Duane said, mimicking Dad's gesture.

I could see my eyelids pulling down like red window shades, and my jaw started aching. I was already dreaming, running through the Arboretum, stopping at Gormely's, meeting the no-arm drummer there. "Ma, I'd like to be excused," I said. "I'm pretty beat."

Ma sighed and nodded, disappointed. Always disappointed. Dad threw me a look.

As I walked to my room, I heard Jerry behind me. "I *like* the quiet one," he said.

After that one, Dad started hitting us with more sneak attacks, usually not telling us more than twelve hours in advance that he was hauling one home. He was trying to avoid Duane getting all revved up for them and me getting all revved down.

"A biggie," my Dad said, pointing a long finger into my face as I tried to wake up. "Tonight, for dinner, at our humble table. A big one, boy. And you of all people should look forward to it."

I rubbed my eyes, started to sit up, but couldn't quite manage it just yet. So I just lay there as I spoke.

"Who is it, Dad?" I think I sounded like I didn't care, but I was just sleepy.

Grinning, oddly triumphant, he backed out of my room, still pointing. He got his eyebrows into huge arches, like the ones clowns paint over their eyes that are supposed to look jolly but are more frightening.

"A big one. You just be there, boy," he said.

Dad was long gone by the time I actually got out of the rack and made it to the table. Duane was there, chowing, listening to his headphones and ignoring my mother as she served him.

"G'morning, hockey face," he said. Duane had been having one fine time with my injuries, especially the blue, orange, brown bruise splotching its way across my upper face. My mother got a lot less out of it, particularly my decision not to replace the missing teeth.

"Stop it, Duane," she said, looking not at him but at me. "Bad enough he looks like a rotten old jack-o'-lantern; you don't have to call so much attention to it."

"Oh classic, Ma," he said. "Let's not call attention to it. Then nobody will know. It'll be our little secret."

She didn't acknowledge him as she set a plate down in front of me.

"Who's Dad bringing home tonight, Ma?" I said.

"Probably the guy who invented the glow-in-the-dark flea collar," Duane jumped in.

"Pay no attention," Ma said.

"Or maybe the guy who wears the duck suit at Washington State games. Or the triangle player in the marching band."

"Shut up, Duane," I said, laughing.

"Shut up, Duane." Ma didn't laugh. She glared at him. Stared him down, like if he said one more word he was going to have to go at it with her. This was pretty intense, since she was so afraid of Duane most of the time. He backed off, popping a whole hard-boiled egg into his mouth before disappearing out the back door.

"I don't know who it is, Eric," she said. "All I know is that it's someone your father thinks is very important, and someone he thinks you, in particular, will want to meet." She stood with her arms folded, trying to sound enthusiastic, trying to sound like she believed. But it was becoming harder and harder for her to pull it off. This was one of the very few programs they agreed upon, this parading of role models to try and light my fire. But she could barely conceal the weariness inside her, and the voice that wanted to say "He's a loser."

"So try not to be late tonight, will you, Eric?" She sighed. I didn't say anything. I ate. She cleaned. I left.

"Yo, Animal," Tom Burris called to me as I slumped down in my desk. Tom Burris is on my hockey team. The coach's son. Not much of a player. Not much of a human being. It was Tom Burris I was swinging at, I suddenly recall, when I hit that other kid on the melon with my new Christian Brothers stick. Should have hit Tom Burris. Would have felt really good, and his father would have thrown me off the team.

"This came for you at my house, Animal. It's from Canada." He passed me an envelope addressed to me, care of the coach. The envelope had a bump inside. "It must have something to do with hockey if they sent it to my dad. Hey, maybe it's the Royal Canadian Mounted Police trying to track you down for all your criminal behavior."

As I snatched the envelope out of his hand, he sort of jumped back. "You're going to see some criminal behavior right now if you don't get the hell away from me," I said.

When I opened the envelope and pulled out the letter, something fell out. It bounced and clicked on my desk a few times, finally sliding down to the floor, where it bounced some more like a single Tic Tac in the box. I bent to pick it up. It was a tooth. It was *my* tooth.

I read the letter.

Dear Animal,

The tissue samples have come back and, as we suspected, rabies is the explanation. We had hoped to conduct further tests in an effort to help you, but there was not enough flesh on this one tooth, and since the other ten I knocked out of you managed to overpower the guards and escape on their own, I guess you'll just have to remain a mystery to the world.

(Actually, Benny found the tooth as he skated off the ice following the humiliating beating we gave you boys. He thought you might like a souvenir.)

Perhaps we will meet again.

Yours,

Rejan Houle

1385 Bonavista Ave.

Westmount, Québec

P.S. I hope your problem is better.

First I smiled. Then I reread the letter and laughed out loud. When I looked up, everyone in the room was staring at me. I guess I'm not known around school as a big laugher.

————

Duane was whispering from the other side of my door. "Eric, man, you better get out here. It's time. He's here. Pretty exciting stuff. This really *is* big."

I opened my door just wide enough for Duane to wedge his big head in it. "Are you serious, Duane? This guy actually is *somebody*? You've seen him?"

"Sure I've seen him."

"Well? Who is he already?"

Duane started laughing, probably louder than he needed to. "I haven't got the slightest frigging idea."

I couldn't help laughing too, as my brother pushed the door open and rolled on the floor.

"But he looks like Freddie Krueger," Duane howled.

I covered my face with both hands as I laughed, shaking my head too, at the thought of spending another dinner with another one. With another *one*.

"And the best part," Duane said through a laugh-induced asthmatic wheeze as he lay spread like the spokes of a wagon wheel on my floor. "The best part is that Dad's brought him here as some kind of gift for *you*. . . ."

He couldn't even form words anymore, he was having such a spastically good time. But he didn't need to. I knew what he meant. How Dad said that I especially would appreciate this man. Which meant that I would be expected to *connect* with him. Which meant Dad would be telling him stories about me all

through the evening. Which meant I was going to
have to—god—talk. Duane was, by this point, laughing all by himself, which he didn't mind.

My father poked his head into the room, smiled
like Christmas, completely disregarded his older son
seizing on the floor, and waved me into the kitchen.
"It's tiiime," he sang.

"Mike Mackey." The man stuck out his hand and
I shook it. It was a medium-big hand, but when I
shook it, it felt strong and like he was holding a fistful
of gravel at the same time. And Duane was right
about his face—it was rough. But like most jokes, it
wasn't so funny when I got up close. There were so
many scars everywhere that you might think the guy
had been in something somewhere between a knife
fight and a fire. And the lumps—on his jaw, cheek-
bones, eyes, and especially forehead—were not
bumps that come and go like most people get, but
permanent, unnatural, disfiguring things that come
and stay forever.

Dad, as out of it as ever, had brought me a real
live hockey player at the time I wanted one less than
anything else in the world.

"*Former* hockey player," Mackey pointed out as
bread crumbs rolled off his bottom lip. We were all at
the table except Ma, who was making busy by shut-
tling things between kitchen and dining room. She
brought in tiny loads, like the dish of peas one time

and a stack of napkins another, so she could make as many trips as possible. She wouldn't let anyone help. "Just you go on and start eating, men," she said through barely moving lips. She wouldn't talk to Dad, who had done it again by *not* bringing home the celebrity who would pull her up out of nowheresville. Every time I saw her secretly throw a look at Mackey, her nostrils got big as doughnuts.

"C'mon, Eric." Dad laughed uncomfortably. "I told you about Mike Mackey a hundred times. "This guy was a crucial member of the greatest team of all time. The Big Bad Bruins. Stanley Cup Champions of seventy and seventy-two. Sure you remember."

"Well, uh, ya, Dad, I remember you telling me about the team. . . ."

"Oh come on now." Mackey waved Dad off while spearing meatballs with the other hand. "Crucial? Me? I think maybe not. You really are a P.R. guy, aren't you? I was just okay. I played my role."

Dad dropped his utensils into his plate and started pushing his chair away from the table, like he was afraid. "Hey, Mike, now don't do that. We can't have you pulling any of that false modesty stuff on us if we're going to get anywhere promoting that hockey school of yours. Besides"—he made a sweeping gesture across the table, taking in me and even my mother, but pulling back his arm before reaching

Duane—"you're looking at a hockey family here. We know. We understand what makes a player important is more than just goals."

Since he was deep into flashback mode—he was trying to drum up enthusiasm for a second-tier player of over two decades ago—he fell suddenly into an accidental moment of pride in Duane. "Why, my older boy there, I remember once, at a game in Syracuse . . ." But as soon as he let his eyes rest on Duane's dour look, he lost the handle on the story. It was then that I noticed too. Duane wasn't smirking anymore. He wasn't ridiculing Mackey the way I'd expected. All he did was stare silently at him for most of the evening, sulking over something, though nobody dared mention it. "I don't sulk!" he once screamed at Ma. "I *brood*. There's a great big goddamn difference."

"Anyway." Dad swung it over to me. "That one there. A budding star. He's got all the intangibles, like we were talking about. Just recently, in fact, at a tourney up in Montreal—you know *that* town well, I know, huh, Mike?" Dad nodded and smiled slyly.

"Oh yes," Mackey obliged. "A lot of nightmares up there. A lot of ghosts."

"Right. Well my boy Eric, here, practically won a whole tournament by himself up there. Lost in the final game, which, you know, is quite an achievement for an American squad. But you know, same old story, no support. Eric had to do it all—the scoring, penalty killing, the dirty work in the corners. . . . Tell him, Eric."

I had slithered down as far in my seat as I could go, and was prepared to get under the rug if he pressed this. Miraculously, Ma came to my rescue. Not, I think, because she could sense that I was in a spot, but because she hadn't listened to a word of the conversation and just blurted randomly.

"So Mr. *Mackey*," she said politely but without kindness. "Just what is it you need my husband's services for?"

"Well, ma'am," he said, "for the longest time me and Bobby, Bobby Orr, we been running the Orr/Mackey hockey camps around here. They've been a big success ever since that first cup in 1970. Of course, they haven't been as successful in recent years, as people more and more forget about what we did. But still, the name Bobby Orr is a pretty magical thing around this area, so even in the bad times we done okay."

"Yes," Ma said, so impatiently that I could see Dad trying to flag her down with his eyes, to get her to lay off. "Even I know of Bobby Orr. He's in commercials all the time, and I hear he's quite a prominent businessman too. One even hears his name mentioned as a possible candidate for state office from time to time. *He* looks very well still. Like a boy. It all makes one wonder, if you don't mind my saying so, Mr. Mackey, why he would be interested in maintaining some little hockey camp? Good friends, I suppose?"

Mackey looked down at his plate, paused several seconds. Everyone, even Duane, found someplace else to look—up at the ceiling, out a window—rather than see Mackey's face at that moment. But he took the hit and went on. "Yes, Bobby is my friend."

The way he said it, it was the saddest sentence I'd ever heard. I felt my face go flush, the way it does sometimes, and if it wouldn't have made everything ten times worse, I would have stood right up and told my own mother to shut up. Anyway, she did look a bit ashamed of herself.

"So," Mackey continued, "I'm sure you're aware of Bobby's condition. He's up to about his two thousandth knee operation. Up till now it was a real struggle for Bobby to get on skates, but he did it from time to time. But now?" He paused again, sighed with a lot of voice in it. "Now Bobby can't hardly walk, and with all his other business stuff and all, he doesn't even *get* to the camp most years. Up till now he left me the name as a gift, but the long and the short of it is that the people who regulate such things get pretty funny about athletes putting their

names on schools and camps that they don't partici-
pate in."

We were all silent. I suppose Ma and Duane were
thinking the same thing I was: My dad can't help you,
you poor sonofabitch.

"I think you'll all agree," Mackey said, "that the
'Mike Mackey Hockey Camps' will have a little less
glitter than the 'Bobby Orr/Mike Mackey Hockey
Camps.'" He tried to smile.

"Just a little." I smiled back.

"Hey, hey, hey, hey," Dad jumped in. When he
has nothing to say, he repeats something a bunch of
times. Then, "Now you've got to stop thinking that
way. That's what I'm here for. We're going to remind
all those crazy hockey-playing youngsters just how
much they can learn from a guy like you. You were a
Big Bad Bruin, for god's sake. Don't ever forget that."

Mackey laughed, "I never have."

From then on, Ma pretended like none of us were
there. Like she was just eating alone. I was burning
up, I was so anxious to get out of there. Dad went on
and on saying meaningless publicist crap about how
he was going to turn Mackey's business and life completely around. But Dad wasn't selling like usual. You
could tell that the promise was good only until we
could get dinner finished and get Mr. Scarface
Mackey out the door. Then Dad would drop him like

a puck. This guy was turning out to be just much too real for everybody's liking, and they were mad at him for it.

"Did you guys really kidnap Phil Esposito out of the hospital so he could be at your breakup party?" It was Duane who asked, and as he did, Mackey, Dad, and me all perked up. It was a funny story, one Dad always loved to tell, and I'm sure Mackey did too. It also reminded me about Duane, and what was going on with him. Duane *was* once a hockey guy. He was absolutely mad for it. When he was into it, he hung on every word of every one of Dad's tales, no matter how many times he'd heard them. Duane used to say that he *grew up* with the seventy-two Bs, even if he'd only seen a few of them play, at the end of their careers. Duane knew who Mackey was all along.

"Did they really shave every hair off your body as an initiation when you were a rookie?" Duane knew them all. Mackey smiled and nodded.

"These boys were wild, *wild*." Dad slapped Mackey on the shoulder. Buddies now, not the leper Mackey was a minute earlier. "You and Derek Sanderson, am I right? Wild boys, right, Mike?"

Mackey pulled back. "Well, Derek had problems, as I think everybody knows by now. . . ." Dad didn't get the message.

"Mike, tell the boys about when you walked

through the plate-glass door in the hotel at four in the morning that time."

In a flash, the sadness was back. Mackey took a long drink out of his beer. "I got two hundred stitches," he said softly.

"You were a crazy character." Dad laughed.

"I was a drunk," Mackey mumbled. No one mentioned that he was on his fifth beer of the meal.

It wasn't exactly Dad's fault, exactly. Those were the stories people told about those teams, those days. You never expected to have one of them at your table. To see his face. His broken face, up close. Dad *needed* his seventy-two Bruins.

Duane was feeling every blow, more than Mackey was.

"I guess I should get going," Mackey said.

"Don't," Duane said in a low voice.

Both my parents scowled at Duane. Ma picked up her plate, brought it to the kitchen, and headed to her room. "Nice to meet you, Mr. Mackey," she said over her shoulder. My father rose, plate in hand. "I was thinking maybe we could hook you up with one of your other old teammates, say Pie McKenzie, to add some name to the marquee."

"Why don't I just clone myself?" Mackey said. From the way Dad laughed on his way to the kitchen, you could tell he didn't get the joke.

"Or even better," Dad said, "when my young superstar there makes it big, I promise you, he'll join you and business will boom."

Mackey stood, Dad shook his hand.

"I'll see him out," Duane snapped.

"Fine." Dad smiled.

I stared at my father's back as he scurried out. I couldn't believe him. Where was he? Couldn't he tell anything about me? My heart was drumming with rage at his obliviousness.

"I'm not playing any more goddamn hockey," I said calmly. I spoke from my seat, with my head bowed like I was saying grace. I think I said it just loud enough for him to hear me. But of course he didn't even turn.

A huge smile exploded across Duane's face, and he reached over to give me a playful slap across the face, and I let him. Though I'm sure he had no idea why, Mike Mackey smiled just as big. Duane went and got three beers from the kitchen, and we walked to the front porch, where we sat for a while. Mackey drank his beer, then I gave him mine.

"Thanks, boys," he said as he walked backward away from the steps. He bumped with a thud into the light pole. "Y'know, I'll be working with your dad, so maybe I'll see you again." We told him that would be nice, but we knew there was no chance of it.

"So, boy," Duane said as we watched Mackey toddle off, the streetlights bouncing off his shiny leather with the wide-wing, 1970s-style collar. "What *do* you want to do?"

At first no words would come. I felt funny. I stood on the brick step one below where my brother sat. I stuck out my hand, and he let me have the last of his beer.

"I think I want to go to the New England Institute of Mortuary Sciences," I said after gulping.

"Come again?" he said with a dancing eyebrow. "Is that what I think it is?"

I nodded. "I want to own a funeral home and take care of dead people."

Again he smiled, and again he patted my face.

"I can see that," he said.

We went inside and cleared the table. I told him all about Rejan Houle and how I hated hockey and about McLaughlin and how peaceful and simple it feels at Gormely's. I talked, and talked, and talked, or at least that's how it felt. And he listened.

Duane listened.

NO ONE KNOWS
THE GYPSY'S NAME

I HADN'T BEEN BACK to see McLaughlin in a week, mostly because of rotten hockey, and I missed going. I thought about it more and more after I went to bed, and it felt better all the time. I could do the NEIMS thing. I could live where McLaughlin lives. I said it out loud to Duane, and he didn't laugh and he didn't run away.

I could do it. The fire in my belly started growing stronger the second I spoke the words. Maybe this was my vision.

I couldn't wait to talk to McLaughlin about it.

The bulkhead was open when I got to Gormely's, so I went down. The single yellow bulb was lit at the bottom of the stairs, but when I called for McLaughlin, I got no answer. The only sign of activity was the prep box set out on the floor. The Welcome Wagon, McLaughlin called it, it was like a bed with high rails or a padded bathtub. It was where they transferred new bodies on arrival, to strip them and ready them for embalming. And where McLaughlin could talk to them and comfort 'em up. The open prep box meant somebody was on the way.

But there was still no sign of McLaughlin, so I walked back up the stairs. As soon as I got outside, two of the suit guys, one my size and one giant, came rushing to me.

"What the hell are you doing in there?" the big one said.

"Lookin' for some cheap kicks, are you, boy?" the small one said.

I understood how this must have looked to them, but the way they were talking was getting me a little hot in the ears. "I'm just looking for McLaughlin," I said.

"There's no friggin' McLaughlin here," the small one sneered. "Whadja do, piss in a casket? Rip something off? You punks are always doin' something." He reached out and started feeling my pockets for stuff. I jumped one step back and drove a punch straight down on the back of his bony hand, making a loud crack.

The small guy yelled and shook his hand all around, then tried to massage the pain out of the spaces between those long hand bones. But it wouldn't work, I knew, on that deep ligament pain that takes hours to go away.

The big one smiled a little. It was a wide happy-bear smile, but he was frightening anyway with his tennis racket paws and beachball-size head. "Come on, kid," he said. "What are you doing? There's nobody named McLaughlin here."

"Yes there is," I said, pointing down the cellar stairs. "He works here. He works *there*. He lives here."

"Oh." The big man laughed. "The Gypsy. Is that his name, McLaughlin? I didn't know he owned a name, to tell you the truth. He answers to anything. Fred, Nowhere Man, Ghost, The Reaper. Hey Tommy," he said, slapping his friend on the shoulder. "Wasn't it you who called him The Shadow?"

"I think he broke my hand," Tommy said, his hand pressed between his knees.

My ears were getting so hot listening to him rag on McLaughlin, I knew they had to be scarlet. My hands were twitching at my sides.

"Hey kid," the big one said, "what's wrong with your ears?"

I closed my eyes to get the picture of these two out of my head. To keep me from doing something stupid and winding up in that prep box with McLaughlin stripping me down. "He's not downstairs," I said evenly. "Do you know where he is?"

I felt a nudge on the front of my shoulder that turned me halfway around. I opened my eyes to find he'd pushed me with one big finger. He pointed to the far end of the parking lot by the garage. "He's probably down working the garden. The sunflowers have been a little droopy, and that gets him upset."

Without saying anything else, I turned and headed for the garden. "Better watch your backside," the big man called to me. I spun, both fists raised, but Tommy was already headed into the home, holding his hand under his arm, the big man laughing behind him.

When I walked around the corner of the garage, the stink slammed me. The manure was piled high on one side of the garden, and the compost heap simmered on the other side. In the middle was Mc-Laughlin, on his hands and knees, gently plucking some browned petals from a sick plant.

"Begonias ain't supposed to look like this," he said sadly. "That man Gormely don't know jack shit about no gardening. There ain't no need for this."

He finished pruning the begonias and crawled along a row of fading flowers, clawing up weeds with those long iron fingers as he went. When he got to the end of the row, where he crouched practically nose to nose with the compost, he looked straight up at the sunflower. Rising slowly, with great effort, he stood to look into the face of the wilting plant, almost as tall as himself. It was drooping badly, stretching for the earth now rather than the sun. He took the flower in one hand and gently raised it up to his own face, as if cradling someone's chin on his fingertips.

"McLaughlin?" I said after he had stared into the yellow for a minute or more.

"Yes, baby," he said, startling me. He'd never called me baby before. Never called me anything, in fact, not even my name.

"Ah, I wanted to tell you something."

He turned to me, still holding the flower but no longer off somewhere else. "So what do you want to tell me?"

I couldn't fight down a smile. "I've decided, I think, that I want to do, that I'm gonna do, what you do. And more, even. I'm going to go to school and learn this whole business and someday have a place of my own, and, you know, comfort 'em up, take care of folks like you do." I took a breath and waited. I don't know what I expected him to do or why he would be pleased at all, but I expected something.

He smiled with one half of his mouth. "Still cain't get along, can you?" he said. He walked to the garage and picked up a broom handle leaning against the wall.

"That's not it," I insisted. "That's not the idea. I just, I like it here. And I could do this kind of work well."

McLaughlin strode back to the sunflower and began taping the broomstick to the shaft, making it stand erect. "I gotta remember," he said, "to take this stick down in a couple of days. All I can do for this here sweetheart is prop her for a while to help her get strong. But this ain't natural. She's got to be able to bend herself this way and that to get at the sunshine she needs. If I keep her lashed here, she's just going to strangulate herself." He finished taping, patted the flower's cheek, and walked past me on the way back to the main building.

I quick stepped to follow behind him. Surer every minute I was with him that this was where I belonged. "Who are you, McLaughlin?" I blurted. "How did you wind up here? Where did you come from? How did you know this was what you wanted?"

He stopped short, and I almost bumped into him. He turned to face me, scowling down from what seemed like a lot more than six three. "I ain't nobody. Understand? I ain't no-fuckin'-body, and I don't want to be nobody. So don't go tryin' to make me into nobody, hear?"

I nodded, my chin tucked way deep into my neck. "I hear" came out like a peep. I guess he could see that he scared me, even though nobody ever scares me, because he backed off.

"Listen," he said. "So you cain't get along. And so

I cain't get along too. But there are ways around it, ways to manage. Don't make it out no damn celebrity sport. I just don't want no one messin' with my shit, you see. I just want to be left alone."

He turned and walked on. Maybe he thought he was talking me out of joining the business, but he was saying all the stuff I was feeling, all the stuff I was here to hear. It was a done deal now.

I had caught up to him just as he started down through the bulkhead. He gave me a glance over his shoulder and smiled. "You still here?" Then we both went into the cellar. The first thing we saw was the big suit guy adjusting something, someone, in the prep box. He straightened up, walked past us. "Do your thing, Ghost," he said as he mounted the stairs.

McLaughlin froze. His eyes glassed over, eyes that never even shone before, as he looked at the woman.

"Evangeline," he cried, his voice a little boy's voice.

"That ain't her name," the big man said as he paused on the stairs.

"Evangeline, from Lake Charles," McLaughlin moaned.

"Uh-uh, Ghost, you're mistaken," the man said as he walked off. "That's Juana from Mattapan. She just rolled in fifteen minutes ago."

McLaughlin just continued to stare at the woman,

not moving any closer, wringing and wringing the front of his loose gray linty sweatshirt. He didn't say a word or turn to me, just reached out blindly to his side, found me, and pushed me hard toward the stairs to leave.

EVANGELINE

"**N**OT THAT I WANT TO MESS with such a clear vision as yours," Duane said, "but are you sure that's really something you could spend your whole life doing? Undertaking?"

We were on our way to school, at least he was. I didn't know where I was going to wind up once I left the house. "I'm sure," I said. "I've done my homework."

"For a change." He laughed. "Oh, right, your friend in the business. Quite the lady killer too, Martha says."

"Don't start on McLaughlin," I warned, pointing at him.

"Eric, it just seems not quite the rich, full life your man's got down there. Y'know, maybe you're just a little blinded by the glamour of the mortician biz, so you're not thinking it all the way through. Granted, live people pretty much suck, but the alternative . . ."

"All right," I said. "I'll show you. Come on with me and you'll see for yourself."

He laughed at me. It was starting to make me mad, the broad range of things that Duane found funny. "Okay," he said. "But just a quick snack, then I'm off. I *go* to school, you know."

So I took him to Gormely's. I was a little nervous, with the way McLaughlin was when I surprised him with Martha. But this wasn't a woman, this was *my* brother. This was a sure thing, that once Duane and McLaughlin met, they would automatically become fans of each other. Then Duane would see, then this would all make sense, then I could really *know* it was right, because my brother would say the one word to make it right—"Cool," he was going to say.

The bulkhead was closed and there was nobody around when we showed up. There weren't even any cars in the lot yet, because it was too early even for the suits to start showing up. "There's no one home," Duane said. "Let's come back another time. I'll show *you* where *I* hang out. It's a place called 'school.'"

I went right to the bulkhead and threw it open with a big sweeping motion. Then I turned to Duane, trying as best I could to approximate his smartass grin. "*I* have the run of the place," I said, pointing at myself with both thumbs. "And I know my man is never in bed after dawn."

"Cool," Duane said, following me. "Listen, do you think I could shake a dead person's hand while I'm here? I always wanted to do that."

"Shh," I said as we descended the stairs. There wasn't a sound in the cellar. And very little light. It didn't seem quite the same as usual, though there was nothing plainly out of the ordinary. I slowed and slowed, until by the time I stopped on the bottom step Duane was right on my back.

"What's the holdup?" he said.

"Nothing," I snapped, then gently nudged the half-open door all the way open.

"McLaughlin?" I said as I squinted all around, expecting him to emerge as usual from one of the places of darkness rather than light.

"It smells like formaldehyde down here," Duane said. "And like shit, too."

We took a couple of steps in, toward that one burning yellow light over the worktable.

"JESUS CHRIST," Duane said, and jumped back, pulling me with him by the shirt collar.

"You're choking me," I said. "What the hell's your problem?"

Duane grabbed my head in both hands and violently twisted it around toward the light, the one place I hadn't looked. There, up on the table in the

prep box, was the woman McLaughlin called Evangeline. Next to her, cupped around her, entwined with
her, was McLaughlin.

"Come on," Duane insisted, grabbing my arm.

I shook him off and stood, frozen like nothing but
Freon was running through my body. I looked down
at the floor by the box and saw McLaughlin's twenty-
year-old work boots, still covered with mud and manure from saving the begonias and sunflowers. Then
I looked back up at McLaughlin lying on his side, his
back to me.

"Come *on*," Duane finally said, giving me a yank.
I shook him off again but started backing out anyway.
McLaughlin, finally hearing us, ponderously rolled
over to look at me over his shoulder.

He looked right into my face for about five seconds, and I looked back, hard. The many deep lines
were there, like always. The stony surface, skin like
sandpaper. But in the expression—where everyone
else always saw nothing but I saw *him*, the man who
picked up headstones and nursed sunflowers—now
even I saw nothing. He gave me nothing, then turned
back over.

Upstairs, tugging me across the parking lot by the
front of my shirt, Duane was shaken, talking quickly.
"I don't know, Eric. I don't know. I'm hoping, I mean
I'm just hoping, that that kind of thing wasn't what

you brought me here to see. 'Cause if it was, maybe you have to think about things a little better. . . ."

I was looking straight up at the sky as he pulled me along. It was a perfect gray, the way I always loved it best. No white, no blue, just those perfect little gray marble swirls to follow forever. A rain started pit-patting my forehead.

"Come on, Eric," Duane said, more forcefully now. He gave me a hard pull.

I stopped walking altogether. I dug my heels in and leaned back, still looking at the sky. He couldn't make me go any farther, but if he wanted to let go, he would have dropped me right on my back.

"If that's the kind of shit you think is cool, Eric, then you really are psychotic."

The rain was now pelting my face. I closed my eyes, and they started to swell. I felt Duane's hand on my chin, pulling my face down from the sky to look at him, which I did.

"Personally, I have a very limited moral code," he said. "But even *I* don't go for *that*." He reached down by my side and grabbed my left hand, which was balled into a rocky fist. He lifted it up and slapped it with his other hand, waking me up a bit. "Lemme take you to school, boy," he said, a little bit of his sure grin returning.

I went to school that day, but not the next. Or the

next. I lay in bed later and later, no longer even giving my family the courtesy of leaving the house to
make it look good. I thought of McLaughlin and
Gormely's, and it made me sick. "Cain't get along," I
found myself saying time after time after time.
"Cain't get along." McLaughlin said that was my
problem. *And* his. Did he think I had the same shit
wrong with me that he had? To hell with him.

I don't know what Duane told my parents, but he
must have told them something, because they tippy-
toed around me even more than usual. Nobody said
boo about my cutting school, and increasingly I got
bedside visits, like a sick person.

The idea all around seemed to be that the week-
end would make me feel better. Like I'd be all right if
I could just make it to the weekend. "The big game
up in Utica, that'll clear the old sinuses," Dad said. It
actually made me feel a little looser hearing him talk
about it, even though it was really his own sinuses he
was talking about. "A couple of hundred crisp miles
of road, gateway to the Adirondacks, big finish to another great season, that's the kind of stuff that helps a
guy see straight, put things in perspective," Dad said,
looking off out the window.

"Thanks, Dad," I said, and he was gone.

Feed the fish, bop a mouse, take a nap, go to
hockey practice. That was the day, several days run-

ning. "Maybe you need a change of scenery," Duane said during one of his several daily visits. "If you want, you can sleep in the 'Jedi room' tonight. It's really quite comforting."

"Thanks, D," I said. "But I'm cool. I really am."

"All right, I believe you," he said, but he kept poking his head in anyway.

The one who seemed shaken though, more than me, was Ma. Somehow she knew that something had occurred, something I considered big, and it hurt her whether she could understand it or not.

"I wish I could fix it, Eric," she said as she stared at Mary from the doorway. "I'm going to tell you that I'd like you to come to church with me again this week, that that could be the thing for you . . . but that won't do it, will it?"

I smiled as politely as I could but shook my head.

"But that's okay too," she said. "You don't have to go that way if you don't want to. If you could only find something, could just find your way . . . I don't care anymore what road you choose, if you could only get happy."

One more in an endless succession of curveballs, my mother was moving me. With just a few words— which I knew were so hard for her—she had spun me around. From her little planet so far away from me she had come so close, so close to seeing me. I wanted now to help *her*, to make *her* feel better. But I had no idea what to tell her.

"I just got some kind of bug, Ma," I said. "I'll go to school on Monday, I swear."

She didn't bother pretending. "These animals frighten me," she said, pointing first to Mary, then to the box of mice. Mumbling and weakly smiling, she turned and shuffled out.

On Friday, when I woke up at about eleven, there was a long black case on the floor by the door. It was like a briefcase stretched five feet long, with a red bow stuck on it and a sheet of pink notepaper with "Jesus Loves You," stamped across the bottom. "Happy Birthday," she'd written, three months early.

I opened the box and laughed out loud when I saw a guitar, a carbon copy of Duane's except it wasn't a real Stratocaster. But how was she supposed to know?

I wish it was that simple, Ma, I thought, not realizing that it had already made me feel better than I had in months. I spent the whole day on my bed trying to play it.

MY FAREWELL
APPEARANCE

I KNEW LESS ABOUT WHO I WAS and what I wanted to do than I had at any time before. The picture was as fuzzy as it could be, but I knew one thing. Hockey was definitely not in it.

The season was finally wrapping up with one more trip into hostile hockey country, Utica, New York. So rather than just quit outright, I figured I'd make that one final appearance, bow out quietly, and not come back next season. Besides, Dad was so rabid about this trip, I was afraid he'd bite his own nose off if I said I wasn't going.

"You almost ready?" I asked him, even though it was pretty obvious he wasn't. He was standing in front of the bathroom mirror naked, as had become his custom, except he had high white socks on with green stripes around the top. He turned as soon as I spoke and gave me a stare. Not the blank stare we'd

been seeing more and more of lately, but a more intense, focused, almost happy look. Just as nutty as the
other one, though.

"Ready?" he asked. "Ready? I'll show you ready."
He grinned and came skating toward me, his socks
sliding across the floor the way Duane and I used to
play sock hockey with him all the time when we
were kids. When he reached me, I braced. He threw
an impressive shoulder check into me, bounced me
into the wall, then skated off toward his bedroom.
"I'll be five minutes," he said.

He had been acting strange, melancholy, dead,
and mysterious for a while now, even longer than
I had. So seeing my father playing nude sock hockey
before dawn was not such a shock, and not such a bad
sight since at least he seemed to be enjoying himself.
What *was* a stunner was the sight—at five A.M.—of
Duane standing in his doorway fully dressed, wearing
his old oversize Philadelphia Flyers jersey.

I didn't even say anything, just let my mouth hang
open.

"It occurred to me that I hadn't been to one of
your games in years," he said. "I couldn't miss your
swan song."

It made me smile, even though I don't like to
smile on game days. I was going to be the only one
there who knew I was playing my last game, so it

would be nice to have Duane there watching, knowing. Making it true.

"Uh-uh," he said, shaking his head at me. "A game-day smile. It *is* time for you to retire."

Dad popped out of his room, fully dressed and dumbfounded. "Duane? Is something wrong?" He looked at me, then back to Duane.

"I want to go," Duane said.

"You want to go where?" Dad asked suspiciously.

"I want to go to Utica."

"What, there's a big concert, or you have a girlfriend there or something?"

Duane laughed again. "No, I want to go with you guys. To hockey."

Dad looked at me. I shrugged. His face darkened momentarily, the look of gloom he takes to work with him. The look of gloom he shows to Ma all the time. The look of gloom he hauls with him to church and to the dinner table and to the living-room chair. The look he never brings to hockey. The look kept getting worse until Duane stepped up to him and put a hand, a grip, on his shoulder.

"I *really* want to go, Dad," Duane said warmly. "No screwing around. You know how much I love hockey. You remember." Duane took a step back and stretched out his Flyers jersey like a banner for Dad to read.

Dad's face softened as he took it in. It was one of the few existing remnants of the days when Dad and Duane went everywhere together, combing the hockey map like he does with me. Like he *did* with me, up till today. Except with Duane it was better, because *Duane* was better. His team won more frequently. There were more tournaments, a longer season, and people loved Duane wherever he played because he was a finesse guy, pretty, stylish, and not at all felonious. For Dad the hockey's been a diminishing-returns thing since Duane quit, and we all knew it.

"You really want to go?" Dad said, all hope in his voice.

It was a quiet, almost blissed-out ride. Dad was humming and singing and bouncing in his seat most of the way. I wafted in and out of sleep, more relaxed than I'd ever been before a game. He was happy because we were headed for hockey. I was happy because I was headed out of hockey. Duane was happy because he was asleep the whole ride, curled up in the back with my duffel bag under his head.

When all the players skated circles around the rink to warm up, I was off on my own trip. I skated the very outer edge of the ice, brushing along the boards, looking up in the stands the whole time. Sure, I was looking up at Dad and Duane slugging coffee and swapping I-hate-the-Montreal-Canadiens stories, because it was such an unreal and happy sight after all this time. But it was more than that. I was looking at *everyone* in the stands, taking them all in, giving them me back. It was like I was expecting a banner—"Say it ain't so, Eric"—acknowledging that I was hanging 'em up. But whenever I made eye contact with someone, there was nothing there.

It wasn't like that once the game started. "YOU SUCK," someone screamed the first time I touched the puck. It made me smile. I was still smiling, stupidly holding the puck too long, when two big Utica goons slammed me at the same time, sandwiching me. I dropped to the ice like I was poured from a glass. By the time I looked up, all I could see was their two big Utica butts skating off toward *my* net with *my* puck. I heard a noise like a dial tone in my head. Again I couldn't help grinning.

I watched from the distance as the two passed the puck back and forth before one of them banged it in past our goalie. I wasn't chugging to get back into the play the way I should have, the way I always had. I just cruised, and when the red light went on behind the net, I felt only a small pinch of bother. I was quitting, had already quit, really.

But they didn't know that. On the next face-off

the puck went to the right winger, my man. He came flying down my side of the ice, trying to catch me flatfooted. I reacted quickly, cutting off the angle and arriving at the boards in perfect time to level him. But he's a finesse guy, not a bang-'em-up guy, and just as we were about to collide, I saw him do this thing that guys like him do that I hate. These high-points, no-heart guys. He sort of "accidentally" lost the puck off his stick, closed his eyes for the impact, and covered up.

Normally, the guy who does that in front of me winds up in Mass General. Not because I'm a goon like people think, but because I hate, hate, for that moment, the guy without the guts. But today I had no interest in it. When his eyes squinched shut, I lightly poked the puck off his stick, sidestepped him, and let him twirl himself to the ice.

As I carried the puck away, I heard something odd. Applause, and *laughter*. I found myself looking around at the stands as I skated, mesmerized. This was weird, I thought. This was *nice*. What *was* that feeling anyway?

BOOM! Suddenly I was counting the lights up in the rafters and guys were skating past me like I was just another United Way logo painted on the ice. But nobody laughed—they all just went "Ooohhh." One thing was clear: If I didn't get my head in this game,

I'd lose it. And for me, getting in the game meant hitting.

I stalked the big guys who got me the first time. One I got when he tried to skate out from behind my net with his head down. Like a linebacker I tore into him, drilling him in the chest with my helmet. It would have been a spearing penalty in football, but this is hockey, so it's clean. We both went down, but only I got up without assistance. The second guy was harder, since he wasn't in a rush to enter my zone without his buddy. So I entered his. Taking the puck out from behind my own net, I rushed the length of the ice, ignoring my teammates (who I didn't like much anyway) and deking every Utica guy who came my way. Finally, I was bearing down on my target, the last defender, and he stood his ground. He expected me to fake him like I'd done everyone else, so he waited to lunge for the puck.

Just as he started his move, I slid the puck ahead of me, between his legs. With the defenseman then reaching and vulnerable, I dipped my shoulder—no way was I skating around this one—and rocked him, driving him straight into the ice. I continued on my path, but the puck had by then slid harmlessly to the goalie.

Then I heard the old familiar noises. "Animal!" "Goon!" "Maybe you should take up *hockey*, you might like it." All the voices of nobody I knew, which were so familiar to me by now. Then the voice I knew well. "Yee-hah!" Dad screamed. I looked up to the fifth row to see Duane, stunned, by Dad more than by me. On the way to the bench I went right by the defenseman, just getting to his feet, but I barely noticed him.

On my next shift, I didn't even have time to initiate any mayhem. The puck had barely hit the ice when Utica's #1 policeman came charging my way. He was only as old as me, but he was already an old warrior, scars on his lip, nose, and chin. We'd met in tournaments before. He was the policeman not because he was the toughest guy around but because he was willing. He'd go to the death with anyone.

He cross-checked me right onto my butt before I had a chance to get set. Then he stood over me grinning as he dropped his gloves. I had no choice. Jumping to my feet, I butted him square in the face, snapping his head back. Then we went. Each of us grabbed the other by the shirt and threw haymakers with the other hand, popping both helmets off like champagne corks. Like a couple of old railroad builders with sledgehammers, we whanged away on each other, trading one for one for one for one until it looked like he was holding a rotted tomato in his teeth, the blood bubbling over his lip. My own shirt was showing drops from I don't know where.

This was just how it went. This time, last time, like a million times before. Hammer or get hammered until the refs broke it up—fat chance—or until the job was done. Blood like I was seeing here was usually enough to get me to wrestle the guy to the ice to put an end to it. But this time it was not enough. As I felt the policeman's punches slow and loose some pop, I kicked it in, drilling him with everything. I became almost a spectator myself, watching my fist, watching his head.

I hit him so many times—shredded his eye—I hit him so many times—purpled his cheekbone— I hit him so many times that the face, the face was no longer his face by the time it rested against the ice.

People were throwing things on the ice at the end. Cups, coins, a battery. At first I just stood over the guy, staring at him lying there. Then, without meaning to, I dropped to my knees next to him. I didn't know what to do, what I was going to do, but I reached out. I took his face in my hands and held it, turned it from side to side looking for something, anything to do. The guy just stared at me, blinked, shook his head a bunch of times to clear the cobwebs, and smiled through fairly minced lips. "Don't worry 'bout it," he said. "I'll see you in the third."

The refs, not knowing what the hell I was doing

there, pounced on me and threw me to the ice. Two of them then picked me up by the armpits and escorted me to the penalty box, where I spent the rest of the period. The booing, screaming hate noise made by the small crowd during my trip to the box was deafening. The cheer when the other guy got up and skated to the locker room without help was even louder.

I blew the blood out of my nose into a fresh white towel. It looked like the Japanese flag.

I threw up in the penalty box, all over my own skates. I threw up in the locker room between the first and second periods. On the floor right in front of my locker and in the bathroom. My teammates, who all dressed far away from me anyway, acted like I was just putting extra tape on my ankles. Nobody asked about it, not even Coach, even though I never did this kind of thing. I was the kind of guy who could sever another guy's head without feeling a thing. I was, after all, the Iceman.

But this time I was throwing up. And nobody paid me any attention. Until I felt the hand lightly on my back as my stomach twisted, my spine hunched, and I coughed up nothing but air.

"Don't do that," I croaked to whoever it was. "I don't like that. . . ."

"It's me," Duane said.

I looked over my shoulder at him, then put my face back in the toilet. "Well I still don't like it," I said. But he didn't stop rubbing my back. And I didn't make him.

"They sure hate your guts out there," Duane said, almost in awe. "I had no idea you were one of those kind of guys."

Now I pulled away from him. "Ya, well I am," I snapped. I sat on the toilet, and Duane sat on one across from me. "It's like this everywhere I go. From Providence to Quebec City. Even when we went to Colorado for a tournament that time, I got booed the second I hit the ice. Colorado! How did they know?"

Duane laughed a little, but for only a second. He seemed sad, hurt, not at all Duane. "Eric, what are you doing, man? It's no wonder you hate the game. You don't need this crap, for chrissake, you can *play*. What I saw out there was disgusting. Not because it was gross—which it was—but because it's such a waste. You're out there playing for revenge, while guys with half your skill are putting the puck in the damn net."

Now Duane had finished the job. I was humiliated. "I do what I do best," I said.

"Don't feed me that bullshit," he said, standing and tapping himself on the chest. "*I* know this game.

I know the difference between a player and a hack. Eric, you have two more periods of hockey left to play in your entire life. You gonna tell me you don't believe you could play them the right way if you *wanted* to?"

I stood up as if we were going to fight. We were face to face, neither one of us blinking or breathing. I noticed out of the corner of my eye that a crowd of my teammates had gathered around the bathroom entrance, watching us. Duane let a small grin crease his face. "You know, I played a finesse game because I was *smart*, not because I couldn't whip your ass if I wanted to." He raised a fist and pressed it against my cheekbone. Only then did I realize he had fists almost the size of my whole face.

"Um, I think I've done all my fighting for today, thanks," I said.

"Good boy," Duane said, pushing my face halfway around with that fist.

Everyone started swarming around Duane as we walked into the main dressing room. Word had spread who he was, the local legend. "All right, kids, all right," Duane said, eating it up. "I'll sign your sticks, but no touching the ponytail." Even Coach, who was assistant coach when Duane played, came over to shake his hand.

I walked with Duane to the door. "How's Dad, by the way?" I said.

He stopped short. "Dad? Dad's scaring the shit out of me, that's how Dad is. He's a whole different guy up here. He loves the atrocity that is your game. Did you know about this?"

I nodded; Duane shrugged. He punched me in the chest and left.

When I skated before the second period, I wasn't as excited as before the first. There was time, now, between me and quitting. And I couldn't just mail this one in because now there was someone watching me. Someone with a real interest in what I did. Not the way Dad watched me, with that little string of spittle running off his lower lip. Not the way the hostile crowds watched for the love of the hate. But *watching* me. I could feel Duane's eye on me.

My first couple of shifts I played nervously. I didn't charge in and attack when the winger moved in on me. On the first play, I backed up and backed up until I was standing in the goal crease. My own goalie had to shove me out of the way so he could catch the shot. He gave me the curious stare through the small peepholes of his mask. Next time down, the winger took the same route, right through me. This time I felt the *four* hot eyes—Duane's and my goalie's. So when I'd backed in to about twenty feet in front of the net, I stopped short, then charged the man with the puck. He panicked and floated a bad pass to one of my teammates.

What that guy didn't know was I wasn't hitting anybody anymore. Poke check. Steal the puck. Pass it off. Clear it out of the zone. I'd seen a million boring, mediocre NHL defensemen play that game to perfection, and I copied them. It was the easiest thing I ever did, and I was very effective. Nobody got by left defense when I was on the ice the whole second period. The goalie could have not even covered that side of the net, and Utica couldn't have scored. Unfortunately, the right side wasn't as secure, so they put in two goals on that side during the period, making it 2–1.

The thing I could not do was hold the puck for very long, because when I did—wham!—I was on my face, or pinned to the boards, or straightened up by a head-on blast. Sometimes two guys would get me. One time it was three at once. They caught me pulling out from behind my own net, with my head down for a second. Chugging in like a train, except that they were three abreast, those boys nailed me with everything. A big lump of arms and legs and pads, we slid, then crashed together into the corner boards, with me as the bumper pad. They all got up quickly and high-fived each other. I rolled over slowly, onto my knees, and looked up as I caught my breath. The closest of my teammates, other than the goalie, was thirty yards away, out by the blue line. They let those guys come right on through.

I shook it off, and a half dozen other rocking hits I took during the second period, and I played my game. My new game. I was no animal. I could see the frustration growing on the faces of the Utica players when they realized that I wasn't playing the goon game anymore and they *still* couldn't get by me. It got easier every time. I could flick the puck off my man's stick as if I were snapping somebody with a rolled-up towel. The puck lay there at a dead stop while the winger flew on past. Then I picked it up and sent it on its way. But I had to absorb the hit for my trouble.

Near the end of the period there was a two-on-none breakaway when our other defenseman fell down at the blue line. Their center and left wing streaked in, passing back and forth once. Our goalie, without a prayer, came way out to cut off the angle, but that only made it easy for the center to dump it to his wing man, already behind the goalie. Skating as hard as I ever had, I poured down toward the crease and dove just as the guy snapped off a wicked wrist shot. I caught it right in the belly.

The center, out of frustration, continued skating his path after the referee blew the whistle, then accidentally tripped and landed on me, both knees into my ribs. I felt all flushed as I looked up into the grill-work of his face mask. My ears burned and I could hear my pulse throb. But at the same time, I heard—

clapping. Not everyone in the building, but quite a few. And I felt Duane's stare. I pulled the puck out from where I had it safely tucked under me, and I flipped it to the center. With a smile. He got up and stalked off. But when I went to get up, I felt a little stab at my side. So I got up slowly.

It hurt to breathe, so I was glad that the siren ending the period blew before I had to make another play. On the way off the ice something happened. I was the last man off, and when I got to the runway, our goalie was waiting for me. From his view, he saw better than anyone else could. He knew what I was trying to do. Without saying a word he slapped me on the butt with his big goalie glove.

That had never happened before, that's for sure. It took me into the locker room feeling pretty all right even though the rest of it left me with a hollow feeling in my stomach. But that could have been from the throwing up. Or the crack in the ribs. When I got to my locker, I lay down on the bench, closed my eyes, and rested. I was beat, beaten, and strung out by that second period.

"So what was that all about?" Duane said. I opened my eyes to find him looking right down on me.

"What is this, going to be a regular thing now?" I said.

"Well, obviously you need me. What were you doing out there, Eric?"

"Playing defense."

"Playing it like a dope."

"Duane, what do you want from me? You said cut out the rough stuff and I did. And I did a good job of it too. Nobody got by me."

"You did. But a tackling dummy could play like that. Is that all you want?"

I closed my eyes again and didn't answer. I was so frustrated that Duane hadn't slapped me on the back and said, "Great job, boy," and so angry at the empty feeling left by my perfect, penalty-free period of hockey.

"Eric?"

"I CANNOT PLAY LIKE YOU DID!" I screamed, banging myself on the head with both palms. Everyone in the room stopped talking. They were already edging closer, to talk with Duane.

"So who asked you to?" he said in a low hum. "Eric, maybe you wouldn't hate the game so much if you didn't think about playing like me, or playing to get Dad's rocks off."

I sat up on the bench, slowly and with a little grunt from the effort. "But what does that leave?" I said.

Just as smokily as he'd appeared, Duane started

backing out of the room. He smiled the sneaky-smart smile as if he knew something I didn't know. As if he knew something *nobody* knew.

"Go find out," he said.

He just kept grinning and backing away out the door, leaving me to myself.

"And don't make me come back here again. It smells like jock-straps in here. I quit hockey in the first place because of that smell." A couple of guys followed him out the door, asking for tips on scoring.

I lay back down, holding my ribs. The first thing I thought about was how my brother was pissing me off, criticizing my play. Then I started thinking about how I'd show him. I fell almost asleep, daydreaming about what the third period, my last period of hockey ever, was going to be like. This is what it was like back in the beginning, when I was a kid at school, daydreaming about hockey all through my classes. I would still do it sometimes, on rainy days or between periods if I'd taken a particularly crisp shot to the head. But I dreamed these days about somebody else's game. About the scorers, the skaters, the playmakers, not about my own brutal game. What a riot, I thought: *My* daydreams didn't even have *me* in them.

That's why I always loved the three periods, when I loved hockey. Anyone who loves the game loves the three periods even though people make jokes like that hockey players are so dumb, they forget to play the fourth quarter or that they play the second half twice. I loved, when I loved it, the two long breaks in the game, to enjoy what had passed, to think about what had gone wrong or chew on the good stuff. With the third period, it seemed, you always had one more shot at it.

I took my shot. And more. Why not? was what kept running through my head. The puck slid to me off the first face-off of the period, and I saw a seam in the Utica alignment. Why not? I rushed, shifting left to lose the winger who had me lined up from ten feet away. Why not? I carried the puck along the boards to center ice where the policeman—back from the first-aid room—came barreling my way. I stiffened, took the hit, and he bounced off, jarring me but flooring himself. Into the Utica zone I trucked, attracting both defensemen. Taking them deep, almost behind the net, I made my cut—a razor-sharp #7—and was in front of the net. I looked right into the goaltender's petrified eyes and . . . dropped a pass to a teammate behind me. So stunned was my man that the puck sailed right past him.

I laughed, the Utica defensemen laughed. My teammates were puzzled. On a rush like that, there was no way I would have ever passed off before. It looked a little silly the way it ended, but it wouldn't next time. On my next shift, I stole the puck from the winger right in front of my net. Crept up behind him, lifted his stick, and picked his pocket. I was off to the races, deking only the slightest bit from side to side as I flew, letting the defenders do all the moving, nobody touching me. Again I found myself staring down the goalie's gaping gullet. But this time I hesitated, then pulled the trigger. He never even saw it.

I heard a few cheers. I heard one distinctive whistle that sounded like "Pop Goes the Weasel." Nobody booed.

Now, when I dove to stop a puck like in the previous period, my team noticed. I got a slap on the shoulder and even a lift off the ice, which was good since I was less and less able to do it myself. This was a new game. I hit when I had to, and hit like hell too. But no cheap shots, no fighting. The policeman one time stood right in front of me and dropped his gloves. I picked them up for him and he whispered, "Thanks," his wounds still weepy. I still did my job on defense, refusing to let anyone by, and when the opportunity came up, I went on a rush.

Why not? Sometimes I shot. A lot of times I passed. Back to the point man, who let fly a wicked drive I didn't know he had. Into the corner, where the winger patted a beautiful soft touch pass right back to me, which I blasted home. I was passing the puck off, and getting it *back*! Sometimes when I looked up at the scoreboard and saw it change, 3–2, 4–2, 5–2, 6–2, I couldn't fight a hot, rolling laugh in my gut. For that whole third period, I wasn't alone. I had a team, a team of live, human guys.

Twenty minutes earlier, none of us knew how much better we were than Utica. When I potted my third and final goal, I heard the old familiar voice cut through all two thousand others. "Errriiiic," my father bellowed to the sky, a proud wolf cry. My ribs didn't even hurt anymore.

But when I next looked up at the scoreboard, I didn't have the rolling laugh to fight. I didn't fill up with excitement at my number 4 under the "Goal By" light. My stomach muscles yanked like I was being tied to a stake. I saw the clock ticking it off, 9, 8, 7, 6 . . .

It was all over.

It took me a long time to get dressed, partly because I was so completely wiped out from the game, but partly because I just didn't want to leave. How had that happened?

Dad and Duane were waiting right outside the door when I finally hobbled out. Duane grabbed my bag and threw it over his shoulder while Dad took my bundle of sticks.

"That," Duane said with pride, "was hockey." As if *he'd* done it.

Dad started walking ahead of us toward the car. He wasn't talking, and we had trouble keeping up with his pace. He was only carrying the sticks while Duane carried the heavy bag, and I could hardly walk anyway, but that wasn't the problem.

"I told him," Duane said quietly. "Right after the final buzzer, I told him that you were hanging 'em up."

"No, Duane, you didn't."

"How was I supposed to know? I mean, I knew it was important to him, but I had no idea . . . You should have seen him, Eric. It was like I killed him. Like I just reached in and tore his guts right out. You know, if it's this bad, I'll start playing again myself to keep him from looking that way."

Up ahead Dad was sliding my sticks like a sword through the Subaru's hatchback, probably thinking about how it would be for the last time. "You won't have to do that, Duane," I said.

Duane stepped up next to him and dumped in the duffel bag. I stood behind them. "We looked like quite the machine by the third period, don't you think, Dad?"

He turned around and sat on the lip of the hatchback. "Might have been the best hockey I've ever seen."

"*Not*," Duane laughed, tapping himself in the chest.

Dad waved him off. "I was very proud, Eric. Very proud."

"Ya, well, it turns out I'm a lot more useful to the team when I'm not in the penalty box."

Dad stood, turned, and shut the hatch. When he spoke, he sounded a little guilty. "You're right, Eric. You shouldn't be in the penalty box."

Duane was opening the passenger-side door, about to fold himself into the backseat for his homeward-bound nap. "Listen, it was a good ride, right? It's nice to be able to go out with a sweet win."

"Ya," I said, standing right next to Duane but looking across the car's roof at Dad. "But winning in Montreal would be sweeter."

Very cautiously, Dad asked, "Montreal? You're going to be in Montreal next year? You're going to be playing?"

I took a breath. "Tell you the truth, I don't know if I am."

He took the hit silently. Then I surprised all three of us.

"But I don't know that I'm not, either."

"All *right*," Dad cheered, drawing his own conclusion. "Here's what I think you need to work—"

I put up both hands to stop him, even though he was making me laugh. "But right now, as of this moment, it's off-season. I don't want to talk about it. I can't."

He nodded happily. "Fair enough," he said, and got into the car. Then Duane followed, climbing into the back.

I eased into the front seat next to my father. "All I want to do right now," I said, "is go home and play my guitar for a couple of months."

"What?" they both yelled. Dad started the car and raced the engine. He looked nervous, staring at the windshield, then at me, then back at Duane.

"Request *denied*," he snapped.

"I'm not making any requests, Dad. I'm just letting you know what I'm thinking about. I thought you should know."

"Whoa, whoa, whoa, whoa," Duane said from behind me. "Eric, if I know one thing in this world, then this is the thing I know. You ain't no guitar player."

I turned around to face him. "D, tell me something once and for all. *Do* you know one thing in this world?"

"You finally asked." He laughed. "Nah, that's just something I say."

But Dad wasn't laughing. Or talking. I watched his

face as he peeled out of the parking lot, drove the small side roads too fast, and took the ramp to the highway like he was launching us all to the moon. He made angry faces that melted into scared faces that melted into lost faces. He was afraid I was going to be Duane—which I wasn't. He was afraid he'd lost control of me—which he had.

The whole question of me was making him nuts. But I couldn't fix that for him, because I didn't have an answer. If he had to go nuts, though, he'd have to go without me.